Dearly Beloved

S. L. Sumner

Published by S. L. Sumner, 2025.

DEARLY BELOVED

First edition. June 23, 2025.

Copyright © 2025 S. L. Sumner.

ISBN: 979-8999286611

Written by S. L. Sumner.

For Richard, a dreamer

"All my heart is yours, sir: it belongs to you; and with you it would remain, were fate to exile the rest of me from your presence forever." - Jane Eyre

Chapter 1

WEDNESDAY

Mile followed tedious mile and Michael thought they would never get there. He sincerely hoped his holiday would not be as boring as the long drive had been but it wasn't likely. Perhaps if he hadn't been determined to make the ten-hour drive in a single day they could have meandered along a more scenic route as Sarah had suggested. They were on their way to a destination wedding venue at an historic plantation in Georgia. His practical mind had never quite come to terms with traveling hundreds of miles from home to wed in unfamiliar surroundings, but here he was traveling just to attend.

"How do "*we*" know Lynda again?" he asked.

His wife Sarah closed the book she had been reading and sighed, fully aware that Michael had only met Lynda Fuller once briefly. "She's the director of programming for the library. We've worked together for years. I haven't met the groom, but they've been dating for a while now and she seems happy. I've suffered with her through a couple of breakups and she really takes it hard. After the last one she swore she'd never find someone and *never* get married, yet she's been planning the perfect wedding for years."

"Who plans a wedding without a groom?" asked Michael. "Well, apparently, Lynda does," he added, answering his own question.

"A wedding is a wedding, dear. Once you have it planned you can just insert the groom where needed," offered Sarah with mock seriousness.

Michael rolled his crystal blue eyes. "Yes, I'm sure the groom can just be cut-and-pasted into place."

"Exactly dear," replied Sarah still feigning her serious tone. She dropped it when she added, "Don't worry, you'll have a good time. Besides, I thought you were looking for something different and a break from the routine at work." Michael was an accountant, not a glamorous vocation, but one that suited his facility with numbers and spreadsheets. It might be boring to some, but he liked the detail work and enjoyed presenting his findings to companies. He mostly worked with audits and always challenged himself to identify ways companies could improve earnings and eliminate waste. Still, work is work and although he was happy to get a few days off, he wasn't thrilled to be spending it at a stranger's wedding.

"I won't know anyone." It was almost a pout.

"Handsome fella like you? Won't be long before you attract the attention of a scintillating conversationalist. Besides, you know *me* and I'll introduce you around. We both know you are more than capable of mingling and making small talk," she said encouragingly before adding, "I'm looking forward to seeing this place. It looks quite fancy on the website." She said the word "fancy" as if she were a small-town girl impressed by the finer things in life. Michael ignored her emphasis on the fancy, focusing instead on the heat.

"Who gets married on a Georgia plantation in July? It'll be hot as hell."

2

"I'm quite sure they have discovered air conditioning in Georgia. Besides, she's opted for an indoor ceremony and reception." Sarah pushed her book into the tote bag at her feet and turned her attention to Michael. "You're not really worried about the weekend, are you?"

Michael glanced over at her; he always liked her profile which revealed that adorable little turned up nose. Attitude adjusted, he sighed and admitted to himself that he hadn't protested much when the wedding invitation came and knew he shouldn't be complaining now that they had practically arrived at their destination.

"No, of course not," then deciding to change the topic he asked, "So, what did *we* choose as a wedding gift for the happy couple?"

"Oh, well, I haven't had time to shop properly so I just picked up a card. We can write them a check."

This was a bit of a surprise to Michael. He had assumed that this detail would have been tended to almost immediately after the wedding was announced.

"Really?" he said "Gee, that seems a little impersonal."

Sarah shot him a look.

"I just mean, uh, they are two established households coming together and you usually enjoy choosing a thoughtful wedding, or, new baby, or milestone anniversary gift," he could have continued the list to include birthdays, house-warming, new puppies, etc. because Sarah's shopping sprees were almost always gifts for someone else; she rarely shopped for herself.

"In one-half mile take the exit right," directed the GPS from Michael's phone.

"Well, we're practically there now, what else can we do?" Sarah said sourly.

Michael moved into the right lane and exited the interstate.

"Turn right, then continue for five miles," prompted the GPS.

Michael turned left.

"Where are you going?" Sarah wanted to know. She still sounded miffed.

"I have an idea," said Michael. He had noticed a weathered and faded sign just before the exit ramp. Annabelle's Antiques was only a three-mile detour if it was still in business. Maybe they could browse and find something in keeping with the plantation setting. He said no more to Sarah in case it didn't work out. And, uncharacteristically, Sarah did not press for more information.

Annabelle's Antiques was still in operation. Michael parked the car and unfolded his six-foot, four-inch frame from the driver's seat. He noticed how good it felt to be out from behind the steering wheel and stretched to work out some of the stiffness.

The store was a mix of antiques and souvenirs. Sarah strolled the aisles picking up the odd item for closer inspection. She was considering a lovely cut crystal vase but wasn't quite ready to commit. Michael suspected she might linger over her choice now that she had a chance to choose something truly special. He also knew she would not want his opinion: gift-giving of this nature was traditionally something she liked to do herself. He left her to her shopping and wandered near a selection of jewelry thinking it might be romantic to pick up a small gift for Sarah. Weddings often brought out the mushy in Michael.

He chose a pretty set of silver hummingbird earrings marked $35.00 and was on his way to the cashier when a cameo brooch caught his eye. Sarah rarely wore pins but, somehow, it was just too pretty to pass up. He returned the earrings to the woman behind the counter and pointed out the brooch he was drawn to.

"May I see that one?" he asked.

"Certainly, this is a lovely piece," said the woman as she unlocked the glass case and removed the cameo. "It's a yellow gold pendant with an ivory cameo dating from the 1850s. The detailed carved roses and leaves bouquet make it particularly unique. The simple frame is 14 karat gold and the back is engraved with the initials "L.F." It has been authenticated as a piece from the local Fairchild Estate."

"Hmmm, she doesn't really wear pins..." mused Michael.

"Oh, well look at the back. See? There's a place to thread a chain if you want to convert it to a necklace." She flipped it over to show him and offered it to him for a closer look.

Michael held the cameo and ran his fingers over the engraved initials on the back. He flipped it over to examine the carved roses again. He thought he had never seen anything more perfect for his Sarah. "How much is it?" he asked.

"$228.00."

"Ah, I see," he said and started to return it.

"Are you familiar with the Fairchild Estate?" she asked, "it's local and they call it The Southern Oak Plantation these days."

"Oh!" said Michael surprised by this unexpected revelation, "I'm pretty sure that's the name of the place we're heading to. A friend of my wife's is getting married there this weekend."

"Yes, they are a wedding venue now," she said somewhat dismissively, almost as though its current status was a big step down from its former glory. After a beat she brightened and refocused on the possible sale. "How fitting to have selected a piece from the estate! You know, I might be able to take a little off the price because it doesn't have its original case. How does $190.00 sound?" she offered.

Frankly, it still sounded about $140.00 more than he had considered for a spontaneous gift, still, he was intrigued at the thought of it having belonged to a family member of the plantation. He thought the fine detail work on the carved roses was exquisite. A small part of his mind was wondering about how strongly he was drawn to it and was appalled at the idea of how easily he was considering the unplanned expenditure of funds. That same part of him was astounded to hear himself say, "Do you take credit cards?"

"Of course," said the woman helpfully. "Just let me get it wrapped for you and I'll meet you at the register. I assume this is meant as a gift?"

He had concluded the transaction, also picking up a pecan log and bottle of soda which were conveniently placed near the register for the impulse buyer, when Sarah came to the front of the shop carrying the crystal vase. He quickly pocketed the neatly gift-wrapped package with a wink to the cashier.

"Oh, I see you've been shopping, too," noted Sarah with a nod to his newly purchased snacks.

"Well, I had to pass the time somehow, didn't I?"

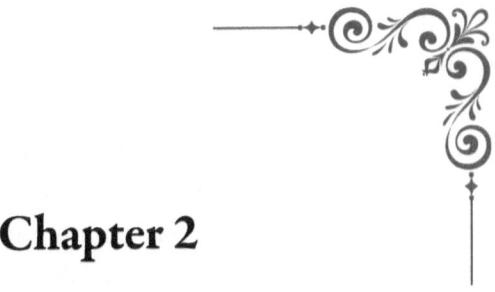

Chapter 2

The approach to the Southern Oak Plantation was picture perfect. Stately trees dripping with Spanish moss lined a winding driveway and provided dappled shade. Nearer to the house flower gardens of dahlias, zinnias, and bachelor buttons combined in an explosion of color. The lawns were meticulously manicured and sloped in a gentle rise toward the mansion.

"It says to follow the signs for 'guests', off to your right," Sarah offered consulting the glossy brochure that accompanied the wedding invitation.

Michael followed the driveway around to the side of the main house. A charming carriage house with a covered drive was marked with a sandwich board sign that read Welcome Guests of the Fuller/Stokes Wedding. He had just begun to pull suitcases from the trunk when he was stopped by a young man.

"Ah'll take care of that for you suh, if you'll allow me."

"You don't have to ask me twice," smiled Michael stepping away from the trunk.

The young man who introduced himself as Jonah effortlessly pulled the suitcases from the trunk, loaded them onto a polished brass bellman cart and escorted them into the carriage house. As he worked, he began to tell them a little about the property.

"Building for Southern Oak began in 1798 and wasn't completed until early 1802. The Fairchild family resided here for many generations, even during the Civil War. The property was ravaged by Yankees and carpetbaggers, but the family managed to hold on to the homestead even though it wasn't much of a plantation after the war years. John Fairchild was forced to sell off large parcels of farmland and he handled most of the repairs himself. The Fairchild family still owns the estate, although they haven't resided on the property since 1941 when another war changed their priorities. It was turned into an inn after World War II and became a destination wedding venue in 2009. There are those who say that this latest incarnation of the estate is not welcomed by everyone. There have even been some unusual ..."

"Jonah! What the devil is keeping you? Are you talking their ears off before they even get through the door?"

This was from the heavy-set woman at the check-in desk. She was dressed in an antebellum style befitting a matron with a starched collar and black cotton dress. She introduced herself as Phoebe and after checking them in she gave them both sweet tea in large, heavy glasses. It would seem that the carriage house had been repurposed and acted as a sort of lobby for guests staying in the cottages on the plantation itself. Phoebe explained that cars were not driven past the entry way on the premises, but would be valet parked and could be accessed at the carriage house should they wish to leave the plantation to explore the local area. She provided a map of the plantation and pointed out their cottage which was just a short walk away.

"Welcome to The Southern Oak Plantation," Phoebe said, flashing a warm smile that revealed a small, but noticeable gap between her two front teeth. "Please leave your car keys with Jonah and he will see that your bags are brought to your cottage. You are welcome to take your tea along with you. You'll need it on a day as warm as it is today. Let's see, Mr. and Mrs. Daniels, we have you in the Magnolia cottage." She handed Michael two keys as she spoke.

"Do you know what time the guests are meeting for the welcome dinner?" asked Sarah, while Michael studied his glass of tea warily.

"It's this evening at seven. You'll find the entire weekend's itinerary in your cottage. There's also a phone, just press O to reach us in the carriage house in case you need anything," replied Phoebe helpfully.

As soon as they were out of earshot Michael muttered, "I hate tea, sweet or otherwise. Why couldn't they just offer a nice bottled water?" He held his glass away from his body as though he wouldn't want it to get too close.

"I may be wrong, but, I think, when you are in Georgia iced tea is always sweetened unless you request otherwise. I'm not a fan either, still, it is nice and cold," said Sarah.

"You can have mine, I can't drink this stuff."

The cottage looked quite rustic on the outside, but inside it had all the amenities hoped for in an upscale hotel. Michael's mood improved immensely as soon as they walked through the door. He quickly abandoned the offensive iced tea on a nearby table and began to explore his new surroundings. He was delighted to see that the bath offered both a shower and large spa tub; the tub would go a long way toward easing his aching back after ten hours of sitting in the car. There was also a small kitchenette with complimentary coffee which caught Sarah's eye. A minifridge stocked with snacks and beverages that could be purchased had more appeal for Michael.

"See dear, this won't be so bad," said Sarah.

Michael had to agree as he opened the curtains to get a look at the view. In the distance he saw a group of the estates' famous moss-covered oaks near the stables. The view was exceptional. He called Sarah over to the window.

"Well, this is gorgeous!" she exclaimed.

"Yes, it is nice!" he agreed, "Now close your eyes, I have a little surprise for you," he added taking the small parcel from his pocket.

Sarah closed her eyes and Michael placed his gift in her hands. "Oh! What's this?" she added opening her eyes to see the pretty package.

"Open it and see," said Michael.

"Whatever possessed you to do this?" asked Sarah as she carefully removed the ribbon. She was attempting to sound disapproving but failing miserably. She removed the last scrap of paper and met his eyes with a smile before opening the box. "Oh, it's beautiful! Thank you!" she enthused planting a kiss on his cheek. "You shouldn't have!"

Probably not, thought Michael thinking once again of the price tag.

"The saleslady told me that it actually has a connection to this estate. It's been authenticated and has some initials carved into the back, see?" Michael took it from her to show her the L.F. engraved on the back.

"How interesting, I wonder what L.F. stands for," said Sarah peering at the engraving on the piece. "I think I'll wear it on Saturday. My dress has a sort of old-fashioned high neckline and I can pin it at my throat. It'll be perfect!" she enthused.

Michael, pleased that she was enjoying his gift, returned his attention to the lovely view out the window.

"The dog is a nice touch," he observed, adding "you gotta love a place that has a big, friendly dog roaming around."

"Where's the dog?" asked Sarah who had been paying more attention to her gift than to the view.

"He's just over there, see? Near the trees."

"I don't see him," said Sarah.

"He's right there," insisted Michael, "you might want to have your eyes checked, dear."

"I just had them checked, my vision is perfectly fine with my glasses,"

Michael looked again and allowed, "Huh, he must have moved on. So many trees to sniff and squirrels to chase, you know."

After a few enjoyable moments spent appreciating their luxurious surroundings a knock at the door told them that Jonah had arrived with their bags. While Michael tipped Jonah, Sarah found the itinerary next to a bowlful of fresh cut flowers.

Welcome to Southern Oak Plantation
Itinerary for Fuller-Stokes Wedding Festivities
Wednesday evening at 7:00 p.m.
Welcome Dinner
Main House, Formal Dining Room
Thursday morning at 9:00 a.m.
Breakfast Buffet on the lawn
Friday evening at 5:00 p.m.

Rehearsal in the Ballroom followed by dinner in the
Formal Dining Room
Saturday evening at 7:00 p.m.
The Wedding Ceremony will take place in the Main Hall
Reception to follow in the Ballroom
Sunday checkout by 11:00 a.m.

"WHOA, THIS IS COSTING someone a pretty penny! And we're not even in the wedding party," observed Michael after reading the list of the weekend's events.

"Lynda said she thought she could manage it because they kept the guest list small, but this does look like a lot. I hope she hasn't gotten into a financial bind. That would be a rough way to start a marriage," Sarah replied unable to mask the worry she felt.

"How many do you figure?" asked Michael

"She said she was hoping to keep it to around 50 guests, but you know how these things can grow. She was sort of counting on the idea that some folks wouldn't want to travel. The bridal party is small, just a best man and maid of honor, plus the happy couple of course," said Sarah.

"Where's that vase you got for their wedding gift?" asked Michael.

"It's on the table near the door, why?" asked Sarah.

"Maybe we should add that check you mentioned," suggested Michael.

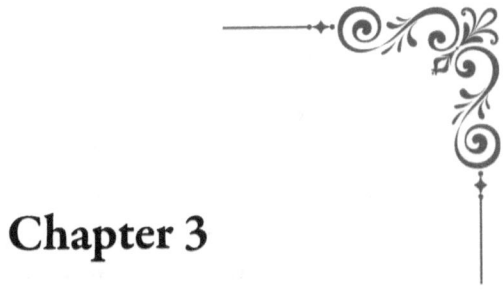

Chapter 3

With the long drive behind him and newly settled into the cottage, Michael found that he was not nearly so unhappy to be attending the wedding as he was earlier. Dressed for dinner except for his jacket he told Sarah that he was going to get the lay of the land while she unpacked and dressed.

The evening was warm, but not uncomfortable. Theirs was one of nine small cottages dotting the grounds. He knew that Lynda's family and the groom's family (*what was his name?*) had accommodations in most of the eight bedrooms on the estate. That meant that the cottages were probably for friends and more distant family. He took in the landscape. Well behind the house were what looked to be stables. He thought about checking to see if there were horses, but decided the walk was a bit far, maybe in the morning after the breakfast buffet. The back of the main house was not accessible being fenced off so that guests could not see the many service vehicles coming and going thus spoiling the illusion of imagining oneself back in time at a working plantation.

He knew there was a lake somewhere, but it could not be seen from his current position. He tried to remember the map from the brochure and thought it would be down a slope on the other side of the main house; again, too far to walk before dinner. He strolled past the familiar carriage house and walked on a small path to the gardens at the front of the mansion. As he neared the front gardens he noted the stillness of the evening, even the birds had quieted for the day. Rounding the corner, he was surprised to see a large yellow dog keeping company with a gardener on his knees weeding the flower beds. His work clothes were considerably old and worn and he had no shoes on his feet. Michael wondered at how the old guy could do such hard work on his knees, but it didn't seem to trouble him in the least.

Curious, Michael took another look at the dog. He had never seen a dog exactly like this before, or had he? Upon closer inspection, he wasn't sure: could it be the same one he had seen in the distance from the cottage? He was definitely some kind of yellow lab mix, but huge, almost as large as a mastiff. He chuckled to himself as he imagined the dog looked like a combination of Old Yeller and Buck from *Call of the Wild* except with dazzling amber eyes.

"My, you're working late," he said.

"It's much cooler to work outside in the mornings and evenings, suh," replied the gardener as he continued his weeding.

"I expect so," agreed Michael. He was beginning to suspect that the staff were instructed to call gentlemen, "suh" to sound more authentically southern. He personally thought it to be unnecessary since everyone he had met thus far already seemed to have a natural southern drawl.

"The gardens look wonderful; you do nice work," Michael told him. He enjoyed gardening himself and knew that a lot of hard work went into gardens as perfect as these.

"Why thank you, suh, tha's mahty nice to heah," he said with a smile.

"Have you worked here long?" asked Michael. He was already brushing up on his small-talk skills in preparation for the evening's activities.

"Yes suh, Ah've been here since afore the gardens were added in the seventies."

"Back before the turn of century, eh?" asked Michael with a twinkle. *This guy is really putting his heart into that southern accent.*

"You could say that," said the gardener.

"I didn't know it was Take Your Dog to Work Day today," Michael joked.

"Suh?"

"I just meant that it must be nice to be able to take your dog along to work with you," amended Michael.

"He ain't mah dog, suh."

"No?" asked Michael, surprised.

"No suh, he jus' comes aroun' every so often," said the gardener.

"Well, boy, are you friendly?" Michael asked the dog, offering the back of his hand for a sniff. The dog's slowly wagging tail stopped as he considered Michael's gesture. He then backed away issuing a low growl. Michael promptly withdrew his offer.

"He ain't real friendly," drawled the gardener, "but he ain't a mean dog."

Michael wisely decided to leave well enough alone and redirected his hand toward Josiah and said, "I'm Michael."

"Well, I'm mahty glad to meet you, but my hands ain't fit jus' now. My name is Josiah." he said displaying his wrinkled, soiled hands as if to underscore his point.

"Sorry, I didn't even think," said Michael dropping his outstretched hand and hoping he hadn't been rude somehow.

He checked his watch and excused himself saying it was almost time to go to dinner.

Back in the cottage he reported on his tour of the facilities.

"I didn't get to see too much because I didn't want to get all sweaty before dinner. I did see a building up the hill that looks like stables, but didn't walk up there. I wonder if they have horses, is there anything in the brochure about horses?" he asked Sarah.

"I think I read something about horses and a riding path," replied Sarah who was struggling with the clasp on her necklace. "I'd just like to see them, not ride them though. Maybe after breakfast tomorrow we can walk up there to see." She dropped her arms and sighed with frustration.

"Allow me," said Michael while Sarah gathered her wavy auburn hair into a fist and out of the way. Michael took the pearls and made swift work of fastening them around Sarah's neck. While he was in the neighborhood he added a quick kiss.

"Thank you, kind sir!"

"For the assist, or for the kiss?" asked Michael playfully.

"Both!" she replied with a smile.

"You are quite welcome my dear," said Michael attempting to match her flirtatious tone. "It's an uphill walk to the stables, but I bet there's a nice view once you get there. I'd also like to see the lake," said Michael who had brought along his fishing gear, just in case an opportunity presented itself.

"Well, I'll scout out the lake with you, but if you stay to fish, you're on your own. The ladies are scheduled for manicures after breakfast and I want to spend a little time with Lynda before she gets too busy with wedding obligations," Sarah told him.

"That's fine," said Michael amicably, "I can use a little 'me time'".

Chapter 4

Michael looked around what was called the front sitting room noting that no one was actually sitting. It looked as though the furniture, mostly love seats, small tables, and wingback chairs, had been placed against the walls to clear the space. Guests were standing in small groups chatting before dinner. Servers carried trays of hors d'oeuvres and there was an open bar. The itinerary, it would seem, was off by thirty minutes since dinner would not be served until 7:30. Michael was grateful for the bacon wrapped scallops and shrimp cocktail since he hadn't eaten since the burger special on the road at lunch. He had quite a little collection of empty toothpicks on his tiny plate. Earlier he had refused anything from the bar opting for a bottled water instead. Now that he had some food in his stomach he considered grabbing a beer, but was not sure it was worth the long line in front of a very busy bartender. He glanced around and saw Sarah chatting with someone who looked vaguely familiar and assumed she was the bride-to-be. They were standing with a small group he recognized from the library and he thought he might test out his mingling skills elsewhere.

One fellow stood out. He was tall, slim, and fair-haired and Michael was surprised that he was standing alone. His plate of uneaten food ignored, every so often he would pull at his collar as though it was uncomfortable. Michael considered it might be a nervous habit since his collar did not appear to be too tight for his slender neck. He walked over and introduced himself.

"Hi, I'm Michael. My wife, Sarah, works with Lynda at the library," he said smiling knowing that wedding guests often identified themselves by declaring a connection to either bride or groom.

"I'm Steve, best man to Keith," said Steve, following the same wedding protocol.

Ah, that's his name! "Oh, well, no pressure then, eh?"

Steve chuckled, "Is it that obvious? I didn't realize how much work the best man has to do or I might not have been so quick to agree."

"Is it really a lot of work? I thought it was just handing off the ring and giving a toast at the reception," asked Michael, truly curious. He had acted as a groomsman several times but had never served as a best man.

"Well, it is if *Keith* is the groom," said Steve ruefully, then in a swift change of topic he added, "Plus, I'm not used to wearing ties. I'm a tech-nerd, we don't generally wear ties."

"Well, I'm allergic to ties myself," offered Michael, "I only wear them for weddings and funerals and not even then if it can be avoided. What's the purpose anyway? It's like a long, skinny bib that only protects from stains that may occur near the shirt buttons."

Steve laughed, "That about sums it up."

They chatted for a few minutes having discovered a mutual interest in baseball. They debated the efficacy of the designated hitter with Steve putting forth the argument that pitchers are specialists and should be particularly adept at picking up and identifying on-coming pitches which ought to make them good batters. Michael countered with a few statistics on just how much it costs to insure a pitcher's arm and his opinion that entering the batter's box was an unnecessary risk that teams could avoid with the DH. He also challenged Steve to name a player aside from Babe Ruth or Shohei Ohtani as an example of a pitcher who was also a successful batter. Just as Michael was deciding that he was enjoying himself another guest walked over and grabbed Steve by the arm.

"C'mon Steve, you gotta meet Joanna and Marcy," he said literally pulling him away.

Steve looked apologetically back toward Michael and said, "Keith you haven't met Michael."

"Oh, yeah, sorry, bit busy just now. We'll catch ya later, Mike," said Keith.

"No problem, Steve," Michael replied being a good guest and hiding his indignation at the presumed nickname. Michael preferred his full given name. A few co-workers over the years had tried calling him Mike, but it just didn't fit, and they usually abandoned the effort pretty quickly. Even Sarah had always unerringly called him Michael saying it had always been one of her favorite names so why change a good thing?

Not seeing Sarah nearby Michael decided maybe the line at the bar wasn't too long after all. Soon he found himself settled in along the wall near the windows with his bottle of Becks. Beginning to tire of standing he leaned against the window sill and wondered how much longer until dinner. After a few moments he was surprised to feel a drop of water on the back of his hand. He dried his hand using a cocktail napkin thinking it must be condensation from the beer bottle. Shrugging it off he settled in an out-of-the way position near the wall to do a bit of people watching. Soon, he felt two more drops on his head in quick succession. Feeling his head for the water drops he looked up almost as a reflex, thinking there must be a leak in the ceiling. But no, of course it couldn't be, it hadn't even been raining. Around the room he noticed that no one else appeared to be troubled by intermittent water droplets. He shook his head, wondering if he had only imagined it when he began to feel steady drops, like the beginning of a summer shower.

"What the hell..." he wondered aloud, looking up first and then around. It was undeniably rain coming down at an increasingly steady rate. His alarm growing, he looked around to try to find Sarah and was astonished to see that the wedding guests appeared to be ... fading? He located Sarah just in time to watch her disappear before his eyes. And then, he was alone in a very different sitting room with a large hole in the roof above him. He thought he heard the sound of a dog whining and moments later the soft rumble of thunder. *Thunder?* Oddly, the entire room was experiencing the rainfall, not just the portion under the breach in the roof. He barely had time to process what was happening and was just beginning to think he'd lost his mind when he felt someone gently touch his elbow.

"Michael? Are you alright dear?" asked Sarah.

Michael felt a strong pulling sensation and some dizziness as the room immediately righted itself. Now there was no hole in the ceiling, no rainfall, no sound of thunder, and most surprising of all, he was completely dry.

"Dear?" asked Sarah a second time.

"I'm fine," Michael managed to reply. "I just thought..." He stopped himself knowing how strange his next words would sound.

"You looked a little confused and surprised just a moment ago. I saw you jerk your head up and then you said something, but I couldn't hear you over the noise in the room. I thought I'd left you on your own too long." Sarah was looking at him as though he had two heads.

"It's nothing," said Michael still out of sorts, "How much longer until dinner?"

"They're going in now, see?" Michael was mildly annoyed at Sarah's tone. She spoke as if she was addressing a small child.

They followed the crowd through the double doors into the formal dining room. Michael was wondering how many of the people present had noticed his outburst. His question was answered when several couples stepped aside to let them pass as though Sarah was escorting an invalid. Lynda and Keith made a point to stop and chat for a moment. Lynda asked how he and Sarah liked the cabin accommodations. Michael appreciated her avoidance of any mention of his "episode". Then Keith ruined it with his comment advising him to "ease off on the booze, buddy." Michael was relieved when he and Sarah were finally seated. Soon salads were served and the evening's festivities began.

Twenty-eight people enjoyed the Welcome Dinner in the formal dining room that evening. Lynda told Sarah that more would be checking in on Friday afternoon in time for dinner following the rehearsal. She was pleased to have kept the numbers small for the first two planned events. Some of Keith's extended family lived within driving distance and, although they would not be staying at the plantation, they were invited to attend the rehearsal dinner and of course the wedding itself. She confided to Sarah that Keith had added guests which brought the total to nearly sixty. When she fretted that the facility had only planned for a maximum of fifty, he told her that he would handle it. To Keith "handling it" simply meant notifying them upon his arrival. Even southern hospitality had its limits and management had not been happy to host ten more than the expected number on so little notice. They advised Lynda that the bill would need to be amended. This, of course, did not sit well with her father and she had spent the better part of the afternoon offering to assist with the added costs and placate both her father and her husband-to-be. Sarah was more concerned than ever about how her friend was beginning married life.

Michael ate his dinner in a distracted fog still trying to wrap his head around the unusual events only he seemed to have experienced. He barely tasted his roasted duck with asparagus and cheddar mashed potatoes. He did manage to appreciate dessert, a delightful peach melba with a raspberry drizzle. Mostly, he was just grateful that the weather seemed to hold throughout the meal.

After dinner there were the obligatory toasts and speeches which could be fun if one knew any of the participants which was not the case for Michael. He allowed his mind to return to the sitting room trying to remember as many details as possible to share with Sarah later. When the speeches ended many of the guests filtered out but some stayed to chat while the wait staff quietly went about the business of clearing the tables. Michael wanted to be among those departing, but Sarah had hurried over to speak with Lynda so he waited near the exit. He wasn't aware of how much time had passed, but it must have been a while because Sarah was apologizing when she returned.

As they left, Sarah was uncharacteristically quiet but Michael didn't notice as he told her to go on ahead. He said he wanted to stop in at the carriage house to ask if fishing was allowed in the lake on the property, but he was really hoping to chat with Phoebe to see if she knew anything about the damage he had seen (imagined?) in his "episode". Jonah was alone in the carriage house;

he explained that Phoebe never worked the night shift. Michael learned that, yes, fishing was permitted even without a license since it was private property. They also offered a small dock with a row boat should he wish to use it.

"If it's there, you can take it, suh, no need to reserve a time," said Jonah.

"Thanks, I've never been to a resort that didn't require you to provide ID and reserve a time to use boats or what have you," he noted.

"It's just an old wooden row boat, but it's in good shape," returned Jonah.

Returning to his small talk skills he offered, "I love the flower gardens here. Do you think the gardener will be back tomorrow morning? I do a little gardening myself and I had a couple of questions he might be able to answer."

"The gardener suh?" asked Jonah.

"Yes, I met him this afternoon. I think he said his name was Josiah," said Michael.

Michael thought he saw genuine surprise in Jonah's face for just a flicker before he recovered himself and said, "Well, I'm not sure when the gardeners plan to be back and I'm afraid I don't know all their names. Maybe one of them is called Josiah."

"You must know him," insisted Michael, "he said he'd been working here since before the gardens were first planted."

"But suh," said Jonah uneasily, "the original gardens were planted in the 1870s."

Chapter 5

B ack at the cottage Michael was grateful to make himself comfortable on the luxurious king size bed in his pajamas and was sipping on a diet Sprite from the minifridge. He was reconsidering what Jonah had told him about the gardens and decided that the old man must have been confused. He did look as old as the rolling hills that surrounded them. He was just about to ask Sarah about her plans for the following day when he noticed she was fluffing the pillows just a little too aggressively. He was a bit chagrined not to have the faintest clue as to why she might be punishing the bed clothes so menacingly, but reasonably certain he would not have to wait long to find out.

"Did you have a chance to meet Keith?" she snapped. Just the way she spat his name told Michael volumes about the depth of her dislike for him.

"Yeah, I did, very briefly," said Michael, "I didn't care too much for him either. I met Steve, though; he's the best man. He seemed like a nice enough guy."

"Well, I don't like the way Keith speaks to Lynda *at all*; it's dismissive and he seems so damn self-important. Did you know he invited *ten* extra guests and just told her *today*? Poor Lynda is spending all of her time playing referee between her dad and Keith, when she should be enjoying herself."

Michael was relieved to see her release the strangle hold she had on the poor pillow, yet not really sure how to respond. This was one of those conversations that needed to be navigated carefully. He didn't want to accidentally insult Sarah's friend in any way, although he privately felt that her years of planning the perfect wedding had done little to prepare her for the marriage that would follow. He decided to go with, "Weddings are always stressful; when people put so much emphasis on making a single day perfect, they are bound to be disappointed." This proved to be a good choice.

"I know, but what if she's making a really horrible mistake? Wouldn't it be better to call it off and avoid the cost of a divorce later?" she mused.

This was Michael's own first thought, but he was glad that Sarah was the one to say it. Still, he decided to attempt to remain Switzerland. "When it comes down to it, it's not up to us anyway. They'll have to find their own way," said Michael. Then to soften his stance he added, "I really didn't have much chance to talk with him so I probably shouldn't judge."

"Well, you heard his toast at dinner. What a horrible thing to say in front of guests before your wedding!" said Sarah. Now Michael really wished he had been paying more attention during the speeches because he had no idea what Sarah was talking about. He didn't remember anything about any of the toasts. He was sure he had raised his glass and paused before taking a sip when everyone else did. He remembered wondering about a smattering of raucous laughter at one point, but he couldn't recall the actual toast.

"I'm not sure I remember his toast," admitted Michael.

"*How could you not*?!" demanded his wife. "He said, 'A good wife is like a tile floor. If you lay it properly you can walk all over it for years!' He's an *ass! How could anyone think that was appropriate?* I thought Lynda's dad was going to either smack him or have a stroke. I never saw anyone turn so red. And Lynda just sat there and let him get away with it! That's not like her *at all*!" Sarah was now speaking in italics and just about to misdirect some of her anger and dismay toward Michael when she seemed to remember his odd behavior before dinner.

"Are you okay?" she asked him. "It's not like you to miss something so glaringly obvious, you usually notice things before I do. Exactly what was going on with you earlier this evening?"

Relieved that Sarah's anger seemed to have abated Michael was uncertain about how to answer her question. "It's hard to explain," he began, "but something about this place is very strange. Did I mention the gardener I met this afternoon?"

"No, I don't think so," replied Sarah.

"Well, he told me his name was Josiah and said he'd worked here for years, but Jonah from the carriage house had never heard of him."

"So, a lot of people work here; he probably doesn't know everyone."

Michael decided not to try to go into the whole 1870s garden origin and he definitely couldn't explain about whatever it was that happened to him before dinner. He needed to think about the day and everything that had happened. He also needed sleep. Sarah seemed to be in agreement because she said, "You know, you did all the driving and it's been a long day, maybe we should just get some rest. I think we may need it."

Chapter 6

THURSDAY

Michael awoke early the next morning and dressed quickly. He wanted to see if Josiah would be found working in the garden. He had gone over the previous day in his mind and he needed some answers. He thought talking again with Josiah might provide some of them.

He passed the carriage house and walked around to the gardens at the front of the estate. Josiah was nowhere to be seen but workers were there placing chairs around the tables that were already set up for the breakfast on the lawn. He guessed that it wouldn't do to have the gardener digging about while guests were breakfasting.

As he was walking back to his cottage, he overheard a familiar voice reciting a familiar spiel:

".... after World War II it was turned into an inn and finally, in 2009 it became a destination wedding venue. There are those who say that this latest incarnation of the estate is not welcomed by everyone. There have even been some unusual reports of unexplained phenomena and strange sightings. Of course, these only add to the mystique that is The Southern Oak Plantation."

"Oh, that's intriguing!" exclaimed the young woman accompanying Jonah. "What kind of sightings?"

Having reached the end of his canned speech, Jonah was unsure of how to respond. Michael thought this might be the time to make his presence known.

"Yes, I'd like to know, too," he said with a friendly smile. "I was also wondering if the estate suffered damage to the roof over the front sitting room during the Civil War."

"Why ever would you wonder that?" asked the young woman.

"I have my reasons," replied Michael.

"That *is* a very specific question," noted Jonah momentarily forgetting his southern drawl. "Perhaps you might ask Phoebe about that. She'll be in a little later today."

"Thanks, I will," said Michael. He then returned to the cottage to see if Sarah was ready to leave for breakfast on the lawn.

The breakfast spread was impressive. It consisted of biscuits and gravy, sausages, grits, prepared-to-order-eggs, an assortment of fruits and something called pecan praline French toast. Michael started with a nice orange juice and Sarah had coffee with cream, *no sugar*, thank you very much.

Seating was informal so he and Sarah found places on the periphery and made themselves comfortable. They both noticed Steve talking with Lynda. She appeared to be somewhat distressed and was trying, unsuccessfully, not to show it. Steve seemed to be doing his best to calm her. It occurred to Michael that everyone on the lawn was taking in the unpleasant spectacle.

"Hmm, that doesn't look good," observed Sarah.

"I know," said Michael.

"You know, it's a shame Sarah and Steve couldn't get together. Look at them, Steve is being so sweet. I think they might make a good couple," mused Sarah.

"Match-make much?" asked Michael with a grin.

"Well, don't you think so? Steve is *so* much more of a gentleman than *Keith*." Sarah was still spitting out Keith's name as though she'd eaten a rotten Georgia peach.

"So, when the minister, are they even having a minister? Anyway, when they ask if anyone objects are you planning to speak now, or forever hold your peace?" asked Michael with a mischievous twinkle.

"Oh, stop enjoying this," said Sarah, clearly upset. "It's turning into a disaster. Where's her maid of honor anyway? Shouldn't she be calming the bride and not the best man? And where the hell is Keith?"

"Do you want to go talk with her yourself?" asked Michael.

"It's really not my place, but..." Sarah was unsure.

"You're her friend, Sarah; it's your place as her friend," said Michael gently.

"I don't even know if I can help."

"I'm pretty sure you can't make it worse."

While Sarah went to see her friend, Michael finished his breakfast and considered that he was grateful that no toasts were planned for this morning's festivities. He sipped on his orange juice, considered having a second piece of the French toast and reviewed his growing collection of unusual findings.

First, Jonah's rehearsed speech had mentioned unusual sightings and phenomena. He believed that for sure, but he wondered about what other people had reported seeing. Would Phoebe know more about that?

Second, he knew that the owners had made repairs after damage from the Civil War. Was one of the repairs the sitting room roof?

Who was Josiah? He said he had worked here since before the gardens were planted, but if they were planted in the *1870*s as Jonah had told him that couldn't be right. He was an old guy, but not that old. And Jonah professed not to know him.

And, what in the world had happened to him last evening in the sitting room? Was it a vision? Did he slip through time somehow? Did Phoebe slip a little something into that dreadful sweet tea?

Eventually, he signaled across the lawn to Sarah using little walking fingers that he was leaving. She gave a small wave to let him know she understood and he picked his way through the tables toward the carriage house.

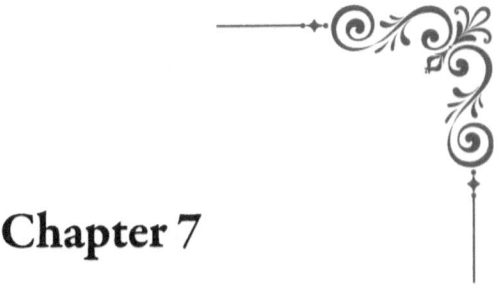

Chapter 7

Michael found Phoebe in the carriage house. Today she wore a navy-blue dress in the same style as the previous day. Perhaps he was imagining it, but her smile seemed more nervous than welcoming compared to when they originally arrived. He wondered, briefly, if she had heard his comment about the tea.

"Good morning, Phoebe," he said pleasantly.

"Good morning, suh," she returned.

"Jonah suggested that you might be able to tell me a little more about the history of the house."

"He said you might be stopping by," said Phoebe, "well, I'm not sure I can be of much help, but I'll do my best."

"I was wondering if some of the damage to the house might have been to the roof of the sitting room. I noticed details in the workmanship that seemed to indicate a repair and was interested when Jonah mentioned that John Fairchild himself did repairs on the house after the war."

Phoebe's eyes widened slightly at the mention of the sitting room roof. Michael couldn't shake the feeling that she knew more than she would share with him.

"John did do repairs after the Civil War. He even had to fell a few of his beloved oaks because he had so little money for materials. I am not sure about the exact nature of the repairs, but you might like to talk to Isabel. She works in the main house and does occasional historical tours of the plantation. Of course, with the wedding I don't know how much time she'll have for you," she cautioned.

"Are some of her tours ghost tours by any chance? Jonah mentioned something about folks reporting strange sightings in his welcome speech," said Michael.

Phoebe laughed nervously and replied, "Well, yes, she does, but later in the year usually in October and November. The locals seem to enjoy them."

"Have you heard about the sightings yourself?"

"Well, yes, but I don't put any stock in nonsense of that nature."

"No?"

"Of course not," insisted Phoebe although her eyes were saying something different.

"Oh, come on," he coaxed "it might not be nonsense. Everyone loves a good ghost story."

"Well I don't," said Phoebe, "I surely don't."

Michael was just about to leave when he decided to ask one more question of Phoebe.

"Oh, I was also wondering about the dog I saw last evening with the gardener."

"A dog, suh?"

"Yes, a large yellow dog, probably some sort of lab mix. He was with the gardener I talked to."

"You talked to a gardener yesterday?"

"Yes, he said his name was Josiah. I told Jonah about him."

"Our gardeners only work on Tuesdays and Fridays. It's a landscaping company from the area. They are not actually our employees." Phoebe seemed a bit puzzled and as a result a bit of her southern charm seemed to have slipped away.

"Are you sure?" asked Michael.

"Well, of course I am," said Phoebe not bothering to hide her indignation.

"And the dog?"

"I have absolutely nothing to say about a dog," said Phoebe a little too dismissively.

"Too bad, I like dogs. I like the idea of a furry sentry keeping an eye on things. I guess he's just a stray. Well, thank you again for your time," said Michael.

As he left the carriage house, he considered that Phoebe's choice of words regarding the dog was interesting: having nothing to say about a topic wasn't exactly the same as not having information on a topic. More determined to have some answers he made his way back to the manor.

Chapter 8

Isabel Pennington hung up the phone with a sigh. A diminutive woman, with sharp features and a no-nonsense hairstyle, she was known for her excellent organizational skills and level-headedness in sticky situations. She was seated at a beautiful turn-of-the-century roll-top desk and shook her head as she considered whether she wanted another cup of tea.

Most days Isabel loved her job as the event planner at Southern Oak, but today was a rare exception. She had just spent 30 minutes cancelling the DJ for Saturday's wedding reception. They would lose their deposit and the popular DJ might think twice before accepting another gig with the Plantation. She was hopeful that she had convinced him that this had been a one-time anomaly; she reminded him that the Plantation had sent a lot of business his way; and, much to her chagrin, she even stooped to a little flattery. That last one really rankled since she actually thought he had mediocre talent and deplored his use of low humor. She would have liked to use someone else, if only there was someone else to choose. She was very happy when the call came to its end and reminded herself that they would recoup the lost deposit by adding it to the bill she would present to the family of the bride.

Next on her list of things to do was a meeting with a guest with a concern. Phoebe had called to alert her to Mr. Daniel's unusual questions regarding the house and a gardener he had met the previous evening. She was keen to meet with him to get more details, but her mind hop-scotched on to the next, more unpleasant, item on her list, a meeting with the bride and her parents about mounting costs.

She looked up to see Katie from guest services in her doorway. She was accompanied by Mr. Daniels, the guest with a concern. Her first thought was to mark his height and then to take in his expression. She was good at sizing up people quickly. Mr. Daniels, she observed, was neither angry or upset, which was a welcome relief.

"Hello, Mr. Daniels, how can I help you?" she welcomed.

"It's Michael, I appreciate you taking the time to talk with me."

"Not at all, it's my pleasure. My name is Isabel Pennington."

"Well," said Michael "I was looking for a little background on the estate and I have a few questions."

Isabel considered Michael for a moment, could it be? Best not to assume, but it was a little irregular to have guests request a meeting unless... She decided it best to allow her guest to guide the conversation although he didn't seem quite ready. Deciding to stick to her tour material as a start she explained that she was in charge of event planning and, when the house was not being used, usually on Monday afternoons, she conducted tours of the property.

Isabel was very well versed on the history of the Fairchild family and The Southern Oak Plantation and only too happy to share her extensive knowledge. She was able to tell him that the sitting room was not part of the original house but was part of a single-story addition added to the front of the house in the 1850s. She made note when asked specifically about repairs to the roof of the front sitting room. She informed him, however, that although the locals wanted very much to believe that the hole in the roof was caused by damage from a cannon ball; the truth was that it was the result of a terrible storm that saturated the soil and caused the loss of one of the estate's beautiful oaks. A large branch pierced the roof when it toppled. The family was grateful that the damage was not worse. The fact that it happened during the war and at the time of a minor skirmish in the area gave rise to the myth of the cannon ball. In fact, the Union Army was not attempting to damage the house thinking they might make use of it to house their officers.

Isabel went on to give him a small tutorial on the events of the Civil War and its aftermath in this portion of Georgia. She said that the Yankee officers never did occupy the house finding instead, other accommodations more strategically placed and better suited to their needs. Local opinion held that the carpetbaggers that arrived during reconstruction were as big a tragedy as the war itself. Many good families lost their homes. The Fairchild family had enough resources to keep up their taxes and thus avoided the loss of the family homestead. They did lose some of their slaves after the war but others stayed on, loyal to the family. They also lost much of their land holdings. By selling off farmland they managed to hold on to the 60-acre estate as it exists today.

Having finished her usual tour guide introduction she then offered to show Michael through the house which he quickly accepted. His eagerness caused her to wonder, once again, if maybe... but best not to lead the witness she reminded herself.

"Let's head down to begin the tour in the sitting room," she said pleasantly. "The house has eight bedrooms but since we currently have guests you will not be able to tour those rooms. The Fairchild family had six children, five boys and a girl, Lydia. Sadly, two of the boys were lost in the war. Lydia was the youngest and the apple of her father's eye, or so they say," said Isabel.

"Who do you mean by 'they'?" asked Michael.

"Oh, just about everyone at the time," replied Isabel. "There are letters written by John Fairchild during the war to his sister and daughter which make it quite clear that he cherished his youngest. There is also a newspaper clipping from 1860 from the society pages describing Lydia and her father attending a debutante ball. All in attendance remarked on how he doted on his little girl," explained Isabel.

"I see," said Michael. "So three sons survived the war. Did they stay active on the estate, or move on? War sometimes changes people."

"Two of the boys did stay on for a while, but the lure of rebuilding Atlanta eventually took them off to the city. Another brother, George, married and moved to Charleston."

"You haven't mentioned Lydia's mother at all," observed Michael.

"No," Isabel said sadly, "I haven't because she died giving birth to Lydia. Perhaps that's why her father clung to her so. Lydia was raised by an unmarried aunt, Cordelia Fairchild, on her father's side of the family."

"I believe I heard that the Fairchild family still owns the estate. Did Lydia stay on with a family of her own?"

"No, I'm afraid not. The estate is now primarily owned by descendants of Thomas Fairchild, the eldest of the three who survived the war. He went off to Atlanta with his brother Robert, but returned with his family after his father's death in 1869."

"What about Lydia?" asked Michael.

"Ah, well, there's a sad story, a very sad story indeed." They had walked through the kitchen and pantries, past the library and were standing in the grand ballroom which was now being set up in preparation for the Fuller/Stokes wedding reception. "No one is really sure of the exact details. John Fairchild did his utmost to keep the scandal out of the papers and he had enough influence to be largely successful. There was a small article in the paper but it was short on details and simply related an incident on the estate in which a young former Union soldier was found trespassing and was shot by John Fairchild himself."

"How does this relate to Lydia?" asked Michael.

"Can't you guess? The young man was rumored to be Lydia's secret beau. Of course, I am partially guessing because we have not found any actual documented proof of the fact, but if it was true Lydia's father would certainly not have approved. I suppose we'll never know for sure. An obituary for Lydia appears in the newspaper just a few weeks after the incident," said Isabel.

"Whoa, a possible tragedy of Shakespearean proportions," Michael noted.

"Indeed," agreed Isabel.

"So it would have been Thomas Fairchild who added the gardens to the property." It was more question than statement.

"Correct," said Isabel. "After the tragic losses of both Lydia and John, Thomas wanted to make the estate his own. He added the carriage house and enlarged the stables as well. With most of the farmland sold off he turned his efforts to breeding horses."

By now they had arrived at the sitting room. It looked quite different from the preceding evening with all the furniture returned to their rightful places. Small groupings of chairs and small tables were sprinkled through the room and along the front wall was an exquisite Victorian camelback sofa. As they entered a young man arrived holding a cell phone which he offered to Isabel with a whispered word.

"Oh, I'm afraid I'll need to take this," she told Michael, obviously annoyed by the interruption. "I'll only be a few moments." Isabel stepped into the hallway.

"Hello?" said Isabel. She was dismayed to hear the voice of a very unhappy father-of-the-bride. Not wanting to handle this situation by phone she quickly agreed to move up their scheduled meeting. "I'll see you in ten minutes in my office; do you know where it is?" Isabel ended the conversation shaking her head. She was frustrated because she wanted to continue her conversation with Mr. Daniels, but she knew the priority lay with the Fullers. Still, while it was best to meet face-to-face, it was also wise to make the meeting as short as possible since she knew management would not budge on the additional costs. She returned to the sitting room to apologize to Mr. Daniels.

"I'm afraid my duties to the wedding party will take me away from you. You are welcome to remain and explore any rooms except the upstairs bedrooms. If you have more questions, perhaps we can arrange another time to talk. It has been a pleasure to meet you and you have my apologies."

Chapter 9

After Isabel's departure Michael was tempted to take his leave not sure he wanted to be left on his own in the sitting room again. He walked over to the windows where he had been standing the previous evening and noticed that he could see the gardens in front of the house from them. *Well, I guess I came in here for answers.*

Standing at the window he touched the sill and waited, not sure what to expect. It took several moments before the first drops began to fall just as they had before, but because there was no one in the room he was spared the uncanny experience of seeing people fade and disappear. Once again, he heard a dog whining and the sound of thunder rumbling. *Was it thunder or cannon fire?* Looking across the room at the wall opposite he saw a piano where the sofa had been which he did not remember being in the room before. A woman was seated on its round, swivel piano stool, her back to him. He attempted to walk to her but found he could not do so. She was playing a tune he did not recognize and although she could play, it was clear that she was not particularly accomplished at the instrument.

His heart began to beat a bit faster as he realized the woman was slowly turning around. He began to notice that her dress, once beautiful, was now extremely fragile, barely holding together at the seams. She had ribbons in her cap which were faded and also disintegrating from age. The ribbons obscured her face so that, at first, he could not get a good look at her. As she slowly turned, he noticed her stately profile. She continued turning and soon he saw it: the ivory cameo pinned at her throat! He was sure it was the same although this version was dirty and the gold tarnished. She turned a bit more and he could see that her cheeks were alarmingly gaunt and sallow; her skin was a yellowish gray with a weathered and mottled appearance. She looked as if she had left her final resting place to go to her seat at the piano.

She continued to turn slowly showing more of her face until, at last, she stopped and was looking directly at him as if she had only now noticed that someone new had stepped into the room. Their eyes met. Michael was impressed by the clear blue color of her eyes. They held him, instilling a coldness like he had never felt before. How he longed for that warm Georgia sun now. As she held his gaze, he became aware of her growing sense of despair. He watched her tears as they slid silently down her sunken cheeks. Her piercing gaze gave the impression that she was desperately searching for someone or something. At the same time all hope, warmth, and well-being seemed to drain from Michael. He tried to think of Sarah to pull himself out of the emptiness and anguish that permeated the atmosphere. The rain was falling more urgently now, like cold tears.

He could not look up, but knew that if he were able, he would see the same gaping, empty hole in the ceiling. The music ended and the woman picked up a fragment of paper from the bench on which she was seated. He couldn't tell if it was music to the song she had played or something else. She averted her gaze from him momentarily and held it to her chest. He then began in earnest to try to break free of her gaze, but he felt unable to move. He had had nightmares from which he had struggled to move or even find his voice to scream, but this was far worse. He wanted it to end, to break away, to be free of her gaze and his own growing despair. Unable to move, to scream, to effect any change in his situation his despair gradually changed to dread and finally, fear. Only after she had broken her gaze and released him did he notice the peculiar pulling sensation and as she faded away Michael started to come back to his senses and his present reality.

"Mr. Daniels?" Isabel had returned and touched him on his shoulder.

Michael started. He was not sure how much time had passed and was not expecting to see Isabel again so soon. It took a moment for him to answer and for an instant he felt like he might actually collapse, but finally he was able to respond, "Yes?"

"Oh my, perhaps you should sit down for a moment. You look like quite pale, are you feeling alright?" asked Isabel.

"Uh, I was just trying to imagine this room as it might have been when the Fairchild family lived here," he said thinking quickly.

"I see," said Isabel somewhat doubtfully. She paused, almost as though she were making up her mind about something.

"Isabel, can you tell me anything about strange sightings in this house? Jonah said something about strange sightings on the premises." Michael blurted his question.

"Oh dear," replied Isabel regretfully, "I really do have some pressing issues to attend to, but I think we ought to talk a bit more. Can you meet me around 2:00 this afternoon in my office? If I am unable to make it, I'll send word, but I will do my best to make time for you."

Chapter 10

Michael was frustrated that very few of his questions had been answered, but satisfied that Isabel had agreed to meet with him again. The phone call she had received had complicated her day and he supposed his visit had only complicated it even more. Michael wondered if Keith had made yet another late change to the wedding plans, but it was not his place to inquire. He made his way out of the manor using the front exit as directed. The early morning coolness was long gone and a humid afternoon was sure to follow, but the weather was of little concern to him now. He took a moment to appreciate the blessedly ordinary summer day; one free of visions and fear.

"Woof, woof!" As soon as he heard the deep bark he turned, eager to find its source. There was the yellow lab at the edge of the garden.

"Here, boy," called Michael in what he hoped was a dog-friendly tone.

The dog looked right at him, wagged his tail hopefully, then turned and loped away in the direction of the lake. After a few paces he paused again, as if to be sure Michael understood that he was to follow.

"Timmy's in the well, eh Lassie," he said under his breath as he headed off to follow. He told himself he had been intending to check out the lake anyway. It was farther than he expected it would be and somehow, he lost sight of the dog. He arrived out of breath from trying to keep up so he was pleased to see a few benches placed facing the lake. He sat on one located in the quiet shade of an ancient oak tree happy to be out of the sun. The stillness around him was uncanny, not even the birds were active in the heat of the day.

What in the world is happening to me? What am I doing? Even if I find the damn dog it's not like he'll be able to tell me anything. What do I expect to learn from following a dog around?

The dog, like most dogs, had made himself very busy sniffing around the lake. Michael watched him for a few minutes to give himself some time to cool off. He was just about ready to begin the uphill walk back when he thought he saw someone standing in the water fishing with his pant legs rolled up to his knees. *Why didn't I notice him when I arrived?*

There was nothing for it but to walk over and say hello. *What could it hurt?*

As he got nearer, he realized that the fisherman was Josiah.

"Well, hello again!" he called out. He was a bit surprised by the loudness of his voice as it seemed to shatter the silence around him.

Josiah turned and raised an index finger to his lips which Michael took as a fisherman's request for quiet. Wishing he had his gear with him he walked closer and asked in a quieter voice, "What are you using for bait?"

"Crickets," said Josiah, "They's good for trout."

"Really? I've never used crickets myself."

Now it was Josiah's turn to look at Michael as though he had two heads.

"What do you use?" he asked.

"Lures mostly," said Michael.

"Humph," grunted Josiah. "Live bait's what you need."

"I've got my rod back at the cottage," said Michael "It'll take me a few minutes to grab it but I'll be back. Will you and the dog be here a while?"

"I never know," said Josiah.

Michael started off but paused when he thought he heard a soft rumble of thunder. He turned back to see if Josiah had noticed but he had vanished. Only the dog remained. His shoulders dropped and he considered two equally unpleasant possibilities on this beautiful bright summer day: Either I'm losing my mind or I've just talked with a ghost. He turned his attention to the dog who was busy digging at something near the edge of the lake. He approached cautiously and watched the dog paw at something shiny in the muddy ground. He bent and picked it up wiping away the mud with his thumb. It was a silver chain with a locket that was inscribed:

For my Lydia.

Well, I guess you had something to tell me after all, fella.

The dog looked directly at Michael and slowly wagged his tail. Michael had the distinct impression that the dog was happy with his find and happy for Michael to have possession of it. He briefly considered trying to pet the dog once again, but remembering his earlier effort abandoned the idea. *Now, what am I supposed to do with this, boy?* Michael pocketed the necklace planning to show it to Isabel when he saw her later. He considered taking some time to follow the dog to see where he might lead, but a look around told him that the dog had already gone as well. *Where did he get off to?*

He considered that it was still early enough to try to walk up to the stables before lunch when he had the thought to try to catch up to Sarah. Now there was still the problem in deciding just how much to tell her about his experiences. They did not have secrets from one another but he worried she might think he was losing his grip, or if she believed him, it might frighten her. Of course she might also be too busy trying to help Lynda sort out the wedding to meet up with him at all.

It was not even eleven am and it was turning into an oppressively hot and sticky day. He briefly considered heading back to the lake to jump in and cool off, but decided more reasonably to go back to the cottage to grab a bottled water or two.

Chapter 11

He was pleased to find Sarah at the cottage. She looked content curled up on the sofa reading her paperback and sporting a new manicure.

"How was your morning?" she asked.

"Interesting," said Michael "and yours?"

"Well, I think Lynda has managed to smooth out a few of the wrinkles; at least no one has cancelled the wedding," she reported. "Keith did provide another surprise this morning. It seems he's hired a band for the reception that the facility wasn't informed about. Lynda didn't know about it either; she thought they were just going to use the DJ and recorded music. She said they'd even chosen the songs together. Keith seemed to think it would be a wonderful surprise then got angry when she pointed out that the DJ had already been booked and would need to be paid. I guess he just doesn't think these things through."

"That's putting it mildly," said Michael. He privately thought that Keith didn't communicate with Lynda well at all, but he didn't say this. He also wondered who would be paying for the band but decided not to go there either.

"I have to say, and maybe I shouldn't, but I can't believe they've dated this long and agreed to marry with him treating her the way he does," Michael added throwing caution to the wind.

"I know! I'm having a hard time watching Lynda acquiesce to all of Keith's changes. It's not like her at all. I don't even know who's paying for the band, not that it's any of my business, but I didn't have the heart to ask," blurted Sarah feeling better to have had a chance to say it out loud.

"Has Lynda tried to talk to him about it?" asked Michael.

"I'm not sure, I tried to ask her about it, but it's a delicate question," replied Sarah. "They met at a library fundraiser. He made a generous donation and told the library director that Lynda had been instrumental in his decision to contribute. Of course Lynda was flattered and grateful for the compliment. They began to date after that and Lynda said he was a lot of fun. That's about all I know. She sighed and changing the subject asked, "So you've had an 'interesting' morning, eh?"

"Yes, I've been learning a little more about the history of the plantation. It's quite fascinating."

"Really? I didn't know you had an interest in Civil War history."

"I am a man of many interests," said Michael with his characteristic twinkle.

"That you are," agreed Sarah. "So tell me what you've learned and don't leave out the juicy bits."

"It's pretty damn juicy," teased Michael. His mind was scrambling, trying to decide where to begin. He decided to stick with facts, at least at the start, and then play it by ear.

"I'm waiting." Patience was not one of his wife's many virtues.

"Well, one of the very juiciest bits is the murder of a Union soldier by none other than the Plantation's founder, John Fairchild himself," began Michael. He then went on to give her the rest of Isabel's narrative.

"So we may have a classic North/South lover's dilemma!" exclaimed Sarah obviously interested. "Do you think they've manufactured some of the facts to give the house a sort of back story?"

"Well, Isabel referred to old letters and newspaper clippings to give support to parts of the story, but she really couldn't back up the love affair between Lydia and the soldier with anything concrete," admitted Michael.

"It tracks nicely though and they would have tried to hide such a relationship, especially at first," said Sarah. "How did you meet this Isabel?"

"I was asking Phoebe some questions about the sitting room and when she couldn't help me, she referred me to Isabel. Isabel's in charge of event planning; she even does tours, including ghost tours," answered Michael. He threw in the ghost tours curious to see what Sarah would think of them. At the moment, however, she was thinking of something else.

"The sitting room? Isn't that where we had drinks last night?" asked Sarah, her mind working.

"Yes, the very same," answered Michael hesitating to add more. Having just mentally accused Keith of poor communication with Lynda he was feeling a bit the victim of instant Karma.

"What questions could you have had about the sitting room?" she asked puzzled.

"Uh, I was wondering if there had ever been damage to its roof."

"Why?"

Now here Michael took a moment to decide whether to tell Sarah the same lie he had told Phoebe and Isabel about spotting signs of the repair because, of course, he had no expertise in such things and Sarah would know this.

While he was making up his mind Sarah said, "Something happened to you last night in that sitting room, didn't it? Is that why you were acting so strange? Why didn't you tell me?"

"I didn't know how to tell you," Michael admitted.

"*Words* usually work well to convey information," Sarah said pointedly aware that she was actually annoyed with herself for having been distracted by Lynda's worries.

Michael ignored her attitude and decided to jump in with both feet. "Okay, here you go: I know it sounds crazy but I had a sort of vision that I saw a hole in the ceiling. Also, I may have seen a couple of ghosts."

"Whoa," said Sarah speechless.

"See why I didn't say anything?"

Sarah sat on the edge of the bed, her book forgotten. She was having a little difficulty seeing her mild-mannered accountant in this new light.

"Hmm, I'm just guessing, but is one of them the gardener you mentioned? The one that the fellow who carried our bags didn't know..."

"Uh, huh," Michael affirmed.

"What made you think he was a ghost?"

"I didn't, the first time I saw him. He did seem a bit scruffy for this place; his clothes were quite old and worn and he wasn't wearing shoes."

"Doesn't seem very ghostly", agreed Sarah.

"No, he wasn't at all. He was just seemed a bit, uh, out of place.
"

"Or maybe, out of *time*," suggested Sarah.

"Maybe," Michael said thoughtfully, adding, "Anyway, I saw him again today, fishing at the lake. The dog was with him again."

"Your ghost has a dog?"

"No, he says it's not his, but both times I've seen him, I've also seen the dog."

"You've been *talking* with the ghost?!"

"I told you I talked with him last night."

"I didn't know he was a ghost last night! Is he telling you anything that may help us understand? Did he talk to you again today?"

"Well, yes, but..."

"What did he say?"

"Not a lot really."

"*What did he say?*"

"He uses crickets for bait."

"Well, isn't that helpful," Sarah deadpanned.

"Oh! But the dog showed me this!" he said excitedly trying to get the necklace out of his pocket. "It was in the mud near the edge of the lake. I never would have found it without the dog. Look, it's inscribed." Sarah examined the locket carefully.

"You said Lydia was the youngest daughter's name!" said Sarah.

"I know!"

"I still don't get why you think this old man is a ghost."

"Well, when I saw him at the lake, I thought I might join him and do a little fishing so I started to go get my fishing rod. I had only taken a few steps when I heard thunder and reconsidered. I turned back toward the lake and Josiah was just gone."

"Maybe you walked further than you remember, when he heard the thunder ... thunder? There was no thunder today!"

"First of all, it would have taken the old guy more than a moment or two to climb out of that lake and walk far enough away that I couldn't see him anymore. Second, I heard thunder when I was in the sitting room last night, too. I have no idea why," Michael began to worry that Sarah was beginning to have doubts.

"So, is the dog a ghost, too? Can a dog even *be* a ghost?"

"I think so, I'm not positive though. He comes and goes like a ghost; he just disappears too. I think he's the dog I saw when we arrived."

"I wonder why I couldn't see him," said Sarah sounding a bit disappointed. "Has anyone else seen him that you know of?"

"I don't think so," said Michael trying to think.

"Did you pet him?" she pressed.

"He wasn't open to being petted, I tried and he let me know. Why?"

"Well, if you had been able to touch him ..." She couldn't finish the sentence but added, "I'm just wondering if the dog is some sort of "bridge" between where Josiah is and where we are. I know it sounds silly," said Sarah shaking her head.

"The whole thing sounds unbelievable," agreed Michael relieved that Sarah was still with him. He paused a moment before continuing, "There's one more experience I've had that I want to tell you about. It was very different from meeting Josiah, our friend, the gardener. It happened in the sitting room again. There's something about that room. I had another vision of sorts but this time there was a girl playing a piano. Unlike Josiah she did not speak to me and she was not corporeal in the sense that Josiah has appeared to me. She looked every bit the part of a ghost from a grave, but it wasn't really how she looked that affected me, it was how I felt when we made eye contact. It was as though I could feel her sadness, it became mine. It was real. Even thinking of you couldn't break me out of it."

"You make her sound like a dementor from Harry Potter," said Sarah.

"You don't believe me."

"No, I think I do, I mean something's going on" insisted Sarah, thinking. "So what do we do now?" said Sarah not sure exactly what she thought about the silent ghost at the piano.

"Well, you could come with me to see Isabel in her office if you like; she had to cut our earlier conversation short, something came up," said Michael.

"Yeah, a little something named Keith I bet," said Sarah.

Chapter 12

Michael and Sarah continued to discuss the details of Michael's discoveries over lunch. They had planned to get the car and try one of the area restaurants but Michael didn't want to be late for his meeting with Isabel. Instead they ordered chicken salad sandwiches from the room service menu and ate in.

They examined the locket more closely. Michael tried to pry it open but it seemed to be rusted shut.

"Even if there was a photograph, it's probably ruined from being in the mud for so long," observed Sarah as she watched his efforts.

"I suppose," sighed Michael giving up on the locket.

"Why would ghosts be reaching out to *you*?" Sarah asked.

Michael was gratified that his wife seemed willing to accept his fantastic story without question and without any apparent fear. If the situation had been reversed, he wasn't sure if he would have given her the benefit of the doubt.

"Maybe because I'm one of the few people here who really doesn't know anyone at this wedding so I'm not distracted by the present," offered Michael.

A knock at the door to the cottage interrupted their discussion. It was Lynda asking for a moment of Sarah's time. Michael asked her to wait just a moment so he could have a quick word with Sarah.

"Go ahead," sighed Sarah before Michael could speak, "I seem to be assuming the duties of maid of honor since the actual maid is never anywhere to be found. Don't miss your meeting, but I want to hear everything! I'll try to catch up to you but don't hold your breath."

Michael kissed her a thank you, grabbed the locket and opened the door to Lynda. He felt badly about abandoning Sarah to deal with problems not her own. He seldom tried to figure out why people made the choices they did; it was simply a waste of time since his opinion would not affect their decision-making. In this case, however, he did take a moment to wonder why Lynda was putting herself through all of this upset. She couldn't be enjoying it very much and where was her support from family and friends and maid of honor? She had chosen a wonderful setting for a fairy tale wedding and truly fashioned herself an exquisitely lovely gilded cage.

Michael arrived at the manor house too early for his meeting. This time he avoided going into the front sitting room opting instead for the library near her office. It was a beautiful room, a real man cave. Polished wood and leather were everywhere to be seen along with rifles on display between shelves of books. An oversized desk and chair were at one end and two large wingback chairs were positioned in front of the fireplace at the other. Above the fireplace was the only feminine touch in the room. It was a painting, or more aptly, a portrait of a beautiful woman. Michael remembered from his tour earlier that this was John Fairchild's wife, Virginia, mother of six including Thomas and Lydia.

A display of two dueling pistols with pearl grips drew his attention. They were mounted on the wall not far from the desk. An avowed pacifist, Michael knew next to nothing about guns, still he moved nearer to them. Somewhere in the back of his mind Rational Michael was urging caution, in fact, insisting on it. Those warnings went unheeded as he walked over for a closer look. Unable to think of anything else he reached out, almost unwillingly, to touch them. Too late, he realized their unnaturally strong pull, but couldn't stop himself even after he realized that something extraordinary was happening to him. The moment his flesh touched the barrel of the pistol he could feel the change in his surroundings and he immediately regretted ever walking into the room.

There was no hole in this ceiling, but the rain began the same as before. The atmosphere and temperature in the library were charged and heated. An acrid smell permeated the air. Now he saw a figure standing before the fire, his back to it. He wore what looked to be the remnants of a bloodied and weathered Union uniform minus the overcoat. His worn kepi was in his hands and his head was looking down at the gaping wound in his belly. He slowly raised his head and two desperate steel gray eyes met Michael's own. Disbelief, shock, resentment, and fear flooded Michael's mind. Battling those emotions was an incomprehensible disappointment and blinding rage. It was as if his emotions were being divided into two sets, but as with his earlier experience he was unable to act on these feelings in any way. He stood, frozen to the spot, still touching the pistol but locked in the gaze of the man at the fire.

The soldier looked young, if it was possible for a ghost to have an age, he would have been no more than twenty. His skin appeared to be peeling from its bones. He was thin, as if he had suffered many months of malnutrition before his untimely death. The blood that stained his shirt seemed to be both old and dried and freshly bleeding at the same time. It pulsed from his body in small, weak spurts. There was no sound, but his mouth was open in the shape of a scream.

Michael desperately wanted this gory vision to stop, yet it seemed to go on and on. He didn't know how long it lasted, but long enough for him to begin to worry that he might not find his way back from it. No one knew he was exploring on his own, they didn't know to come look for him. Fear of his own gradually replaced all other emotions as he struggled against the soldier's stare.

Then he remembered the locket. He still could not move to retrieve it, but he began to think of it as if his life depended on it. He tried to picture it in his mind, the heart shaped locket, the inscription, even its broken chain. As he did so he noticed a distinct change in the soldier's eyes and his own mood lightened. A few moments later, a grateful Michael watched as the specter began to fade from view.

As Michael came more to himself, he noticed that now, instead of merely touching the barrel of the pistol, he was holding it tightly by its pearl grip as if readying to shoot. More than a little surprised, since he had felt himself unable to move and had no memory of having picked it up, he immediately returned it to its resting place on the wall and quickly exited the room.

In the hallway Michael checked his watch certain he had missed his meeting; he was surprised to see that only a few minutes had passed. After taking a moment to gather himself, he decided to pop into Isabel's office to see if she might also be early. Sure enough, he found her at her desk, ending a phone call and shaking her head.

"Hi, I know I'm a little early..." he began.

"It's just fine," Isabel assured him, "Come on in."

"Everything okay? Crisis averted?" he asked.

"Oh, yes, everything is back on track," she smiled.

"I assume the Fuller/Stokes wedding is the only program happening this weekend, but perhaps I shouldn't assume," said Michael.

"Yes, they have the estate all to themselves for the weekend," confirmed Isabel.

"My wife tells me they keep providing surprises which is complicating things quite a bit."

"Well, weddings often do come with high expectations," said Isabel diplomatically.

"Some more than others I bet," Michael offered with a sympathetic look.

"I do prefer to host family reunions," Isabel admitted with a rueful smile.

"Do you have time for some questions?"

"Yes, please have a seat," invited Isabel, "What can I help you with?"

"I think I'd like to know about the 'unusual sightings' Jonah mentions in his welcome speech. What kinds of things have people reported seeing?" he asked.

"It's been quite a while since anyone has reported anything, but I can tell you that many of the reported sightings over the years have occurred during the month of July, especially around the third full week as it is now." She allowed this information a moment to sink in before continuing.

"About two years ago a woman staying in the main house in Lydia's former bedroom reported hearing piano music that woke her from her sleep. A few nights later she thought she saw a young girl with strikingly blue eyes reflected in the dresser mirror. She was shaken up enough to check out three days early. Of course, we don't want our guests leaving us early so we don't publicize the specifics of sightings. Still, the idea of unusual sightings has actually brought in business so I guess we walk a fine line," she concluded.

"Do you believe in the sightings?" Michael asked.

"I believe that young woman saw something that frightened her enough to check out," said Isabel, once again the diplomat. "And, of course, the house does have a bloody history what with the war and the death of the Union soldier."

"Has anyone ever mentioned seeing a dog?"

"We do have some dogs up at the stables with the horses. I think we have two, they are a beagle and an Australian shepherd. They are company for the horses and guests like to visit with them. They are trained to stay in their area up the hill near the stable and pastures."

"How about a very large yellow lab?"

Isabel looked at Michael and hesitated. He couldn't decide if she was impressed or worried by this particular question.

"Have you seen such a dog?" asked Isabel.

"Yes, a few times now, twice with a gardener named Josiah," Michael replied watching her carefully for her reaction.

"You've seen Josiah," breathed Isabel.

Michael could feel his excitement grow; he also felt relief. He had begun to believe that maybe he was losing his grip on reality.

"You know of him?"

Isabel nodded. "Josiah was the name of one of the house servants, a former slave who remained loyal to the family after the war. He mostly cared for the carriages, horses and gardens. There is some evidence that he was close to John's daughter, a closeness that grew out of her fondness for the horses. He gave her pony rides as a child and later taught her to ride on her own. Where have you seen Josiah?"

"In the garden in front of the main house last night, he was on his hands and knees weeding, and again today near the lake, fishing. The dog was with him both times but he told me that the dog isn't his."

"You've *spoken* with Josiah?!" Isabel seemed even more shocked by this information than Sarah had been.

"Wait! There's a photograph," said Isabel, her excitement continuing to rise. "It's really a photo of Lydia on a gift pony her father had gotten for her 10th birthday, but I'm pretty sure Josiah's in it too, holding the horse." She had gotten up and consulted a file that contained old tintype photos. Michael got up to join her, interested in the old photographs.

"Ah, here it is!" she said.

"That sure looks like him," whispered Michael.

"This is the man you saw? Are you sure?" asked Isabel.

"I'm not sure about anything lately, but he does look like the man I saw."

"I believe you."

"You do? Why?"

"Because I've seen him on occasion myself. But no one has ever reported speaking with him before."

Chapter 13

Isabel explained that she had lived in the area near the plantation for most of her life and had heard many of the stories about sightings and strange occurrences. Of course, at first, she did not believe them to be true, but when given the opportunity to work in hospitality services on the actual plantation with its reputation for the paranormal she eagerly accepted. She wasn't sure if she wanted to find proof or not, but the idea of ghosts only made the offer more interesting.

She told Michael that she became interested in the history of the plantation and proposed adding historical tours to what was then a bed and breakfast inn after she'd worked there a while. Management found her ideas intriguing and she was promoted to head of event planning. She began to research the history of the estate to prepare for the first tours and she assembled background for her tour using old newspaper clippings, photographs and letters.

Photography was in its infancy during the American Civil War so Isabel was only able to locate a handful of tintype photographs. John Fairchild, away for much of the war years, was an avid correspondent so his letters were a major source of information. In them he displayed his love for his children with Lydia figuring most prominently. He refrained from descriptions of battles in his letters home preferring to focus on the family and plans for the farm after his service ended. He achieved the rank of colonel but mostly due to attrition as he had seen many of his fellow soldiers fall on the battlefield.

Newspaper clippings from the Southern Recorder provided information about the more prominent families. Isabel had located several Fairchild obituaries, Lydia and Thomas Fairchild's birth announcements, and a few society articles in which the family was mentioned. She was disappointed not to be able to locate any journals or diaries among the remaining articles left in the home.

In addition to her research Isabel had been carefully recording any sightings that became known to her. It did not take long for staff members to begin to refer guests with unusual complaints to her, happy not to have to address those problems themselves. She had, therefore, compiled some data regarding the dates, times, locations and details of sightings and unusual phenomena. She would be happy to share this information with Michael if he was interested. First, however, she asked if he would share his experiences with her and would he mind if she took a few notes?

Michael was only too happy to share his experiences and Isabel busily made notes. When he was finished, she continued to jot down details for a few minutes more before returning her attention to him.

"So now you have seen Josiah twice, the girl at the piano, and the soldier in the study," she summarized.

"And the dog," added Michael. "What do you know about the dog?"

"I don't know anything in the sense that I could back it up with anything concrete, but I, too, have seen a yellow dog. In fact, it took me quite a while to realize that I was seeing a dog that others were unable to see, years in fact. I think the dog was attached to the Union soldier but it's just a guess."

"Does he have a name?"

"None that I am aware of," Isabel answered.

"So what do you make of everything I've told you?" asked Michael.

"Well, to put it succinctly, in a single day you seem to have seen all the ghosts I am aware of except for John Fairchild. It's quite impressive; I've never known anyone else to see more than one of the entities, let alone four, if we include the dog. Michael, I think you must be a sensitive."

"A what?"

"A sensitive is someone who can perceive and recognize echoes of the past, restless spirits, or energy. Some sensitives have visions, others simply sense a presence or feeling. You seem to be able to do both. It's very unusual to come across someone like you."

"*You've* seen Josiah does that mean you're a sensitive?" asked Michael somehow not wanting to be alone in his new-found ability.

"Maybe, but I've only seen Josiah and the dog and that's over a period of many *years*. What I find most interesting is that they seem to be trying to communicate with you in some fashion. That coupled with it being the third week of July make me wonder if they will be reaching out to you again in some way."

"What is the significance of the third week of July?" asked Michael.

"The newspaper article about the shooting of the Union soldier was dated July 17, 1865. The Recorder was a weekly paper and I've read the article several times, but the date of the actual incident is unclear. As I mentioned it was very brief and to the point. Lydia's obituary was published on July 31st. Obituaries were not always published immediately after a death so she may have died much earlier than the date of the newspaper itself. Her gravestone only indicates the year of her birth and death, 1843-1865. The third week of July may be related to her death, I just can't be sure." replied Isabel. It was evident to Michael that Isabel had given this a lot of thought. Whenever she spoke about the history of the plantation, she had all the facts at the tip of her tongue without the need to refer to documents or notes. She really was fluent in all things related to Southern Oak.

"I just don't see how I can be a sensitive, nothing like this has ever happened to me before. Why now?" asked Michael.

"I'm no expert," said Isabel, "but perhaps you have not come across unsettled spirits before now. I guess there's a first time for everything."

"Do you have notes on where John Fairchild's ghost has been seen?" asked Michael not sure if he wanted to know so that he could seek him out, or, more likely, avoid an encounter.

"Yes, he has been seen in the main hall and at the stables. He is the least frequently reported sighting; I am only aware of two reported incidents," replied Isabel.

"Has anyone ever been injured after an encounter?" He was a little embarrassed asking this question, but, as they say, "inquiring minds want to know".

"Not to my knowledge, but the two guests that I know of who saw what I believe was John Fairchild's ghost *both* left the estate before the end of their stay."

"Recently?"

"No, I'd have to check my records for exact dates, but it's been a few years. Of course, my own records are almost certainly incomplete; there are probably some visitors who have not reported their unusual experiences."

"How did you determine that it was John Fairchild who was seen?" asked Michael.

"That's a good question. I guess I can't be absolutely sure, but he was male so he couldn't be Lydia, he was white so he wasn't Josiah, and he wasn't described as wearing a uniform so that ruled out the soldier."

"How was he described?"

"He was described to me as 'in a rage and holding a smoking gun.'"

"A smoking gun that could have been used on the soldier I saw in the library."

Isabel nodded her agreement.

"Any suggestions about what to do next?" asked Michael in earnest. "In the movies they always try to help uneasy spirits find peace and move on. That's why I thought to consciously remember the locket for the soldier – well, partly for the soldier, but mostly in the hope that it might end the vision." Michael was nothing, if not honest.

"Yes, I think that was an excellent decision on your part. Since they are so eager to reach out to you, it makes sense to attempt to convey your own message as well," said Isabel before asking, "I wonder if I might see the locket; you say you found it near the lake?"

"The dog found it," corrected Michael.

"Yes, even the dog seems to be trying to communicate," said Isabel examining the locket.

"Do you think it belonged to Lydia Fairchild?"

"It would be difficult to verify provenance as the estate since it was found at the lake. Southern Oak has hosted hundreds of guests over the years and Lydia is not an uncommon name," said Isabel thoughtfully.

"Well, it was dug up by a ghost dog, there's that," said Michael his trademark twinkle returning.

Isabel returned his smile, "Yes, there is that," she agreed as she returned the locket to him.

Another soft knock told them both that Isabel was needed elsewhere.

Chapter 14

On the walk back to the Magnolia Cottage Michael's thoughts returned to the smoking gun. He had a lot to consider after his conversation with Isabel, yet his only thoughts were riveted on Isabel's description of the ghost of John Fairchild in a rage and holding a smoking gun. He had returned to his cottage to see if he could talk with Sarah but she hadn't returned.

Again and again his thoughts returned to the gun. Was it the pearl handled gun from the library? He was almost sure it was, but he hadn't seen John Fairchild in the study, only the soldier. Wouldn't the guns belong to Fairchild? He couldn't decide if he should try the stables or the main hall or just go back to the library for another look at that gun; he desperately wanted to see it again. His longing was tempered by weariness so he did not, for the moment, act on his impulse. Instead, he thought it might be nice to take a small break, maybe a little nap, just for a few minutes until Sarah came back. He stretched his long legs out across the sofa and closed his eyes.

The gentle tink, tink of someone stirring a cup of tea catches his attention. He looks over to see a handsome woman with hazel eyes sitting across from him on a wooden chair. She places the spoon on the porcelain saucer and takes a sip. "She's unhappy, John, you know how she is when she's so unhappy." On the table next to her

Michael sees the pistol from the library. "I just don't like seeing her this unhappy."

"Woof woof." It is a soft bark, a reminder. The dog wants his attention but he is still staring at the gun. He needs to see that gun again.

Now the smell of horses and manure. A young woman is reading a letter, she folds it and unfolds it over and over again. Its contents have upset her. "WOOF, woof." Another reminder, more insistent.

The girl is startled by the sound of footsteps. She quickly folds the letter and hides it in the sleeve of her dress. The silhouette of a large man darkens the entrance to the stable. As he steps inside his silhouette seems to dissolve as he takes form. He fills the space. He is searching, searching, searching. At last his deep brown eyes rest upon the girl and his features soften. A horse nickers a greeting.

WOOF! WOOF! A warning bark goes unheeded.

A strong smell of gunpowder fills the space. A woman's scream followed by the sound of a body falling with a soft thud. A guttural moan emanates from the form of the man with the deep brown eyes. He allows the gun to fall to the ground needing his hands free to be a place in which to bury his face.

Tink, tink. "I'm so worried about her, John."

"Michael?" Sarah is shaking him awake.

"Wha...?" Michael jerked himself to a sitting position.

"You've been having a dream, I had a hard time waking you out of it," said Sarah, her concern evident. "Maybe I should have let you sleep ...?"

"No, I'm glad you woke me. It was a very strange dream," said Michael still clearing his head.

"Do you remember it?"

"Let me think a second," Michael tried to recall, but like many dreams that fade quickly upon wakening he could only recall snatches. "Um, there was a dog barking, the gun, some horses, and a woman."

"A woman?" asked Sarah, "Lydia maybe?"

"No definitely not, she was older and she had a cup of tea."

"Good, you're remembering more, keep thinking," urged Sarah.

"I kept hearing a dog bark, but I never saw the dog. I think part of the dream was in the stables because of the horse. The pistol was the same one from the library. I want to get back to library to have another look at it to be sure."

"I'm coming with you," said Sarah firmly.

"It's not necessary," said Michael.

"The hell it isn't," said Sarah.

Sarah and Michael walked past the now familiar carriage house toward the estate. Sarah tried to get him to remember more about the dream, but he was walking so quickly she had a difficult time keeping up with him. Finally she grabbed his arm.

"Hold on a second," she said annoyed, "What's the rush?"

"I told you, I need to see the gun," muttered Michael jerking his arm away from her, clearly angry.

"Why?" she demanded taking his arm once again. "Why do you *need* to see it?"

Michael yanked his arm back in a very un-Michael-like way and began to walk away. Sarah immediately compared it in her mind to how Keith treated Lynda and was having none of it.

"What's the matter with you?" she called after him. "This isn't like you at all!"

Michael spun around to face Sarah; his eyes bright with fury. Sarah, was, for the first time in her life, worried at what this version of Michael might do. They held one another's gaze for a beat until, at last, Michael realized what he was doing.

"Oh my God, I'm so sorry," he said genuinely contrite. "I don't know what came over me."

"I'm starting to wonder if we should just leave sleeping ghosts lie," said Sarah.

"Problem is, I don't think they are sleeping," said Michael worriedly.

Chapter 15

Michael led the way to Isabel's office, he walked at a more reasonable pace now with Sarah at his side, hand-in-hand. He was relieved to find Isabel at her desk working at her computer. He introduced Sarah and apologized for interrupting her work yet again, but Isabel assured him that it was no imposition.

Michael did his best to describe his dream but by now it seemed to be a jumble of impressions that flitted from image to image. He repeated his wish to see the pistol from the library several times as he spoke.

Sarah and Isabel exchanged a worried look at his growing obsession with the gun. Michael finally reached the end of his rambling and it was Sarah's turn to speak.

"When Michael first told me about his experiences here I was intrigued, but not sure what to think. Still, he seemed to be enjoying his discoveries. I've been distracted by the wedding so I didn't realize how frequently he's been having these encounters. They seem to be getting more threatening and intense and now I'm worried. Just a few minutes ago he pulled away from me almost violently which is just not like him. And what is this gun he keeps going on about?"

"Michael had a vision in the library where there is a display of pistols. I'm not sure but I think the vision was triggered when he touched one of them. I've already told Michael that I believe the ghosts are attempting to communicate something to him. I don't know if it's best to continue to try to discover their message or simply avoid contact."

"Avoid contact?! How? He appears to have no control over these encounters! They just keep happening to him," interrupted Sarah.

"I understand your concern, I really do. I don't claim to be an expert and I'd understand if you decided to leave," said Isabel.

"Leave?! I'd feel terrible leaving Lynda now. I don't know what to do. I can't understand any of this," said Sarah.

"I know it's difficult, but it's also fascinating," offered Isabel. "Michael has had actual encounters with the more benevolent spirits, visions of the more traumatized spirits, and now dreams. I've never experienced anything like his ability to connect with the plantation's resident spirits."

"But this is crazy," said Sarah worriedly, "he's never had dreams or visions or anything like this before."

Now Isabel turned to Michael, "What would you like to do?"

Michael, who had not been following the conversation closely, stopped himself from blurting, *I need to see the pistol again*, and instead said, "I need to see this through and I think the pistol may be key to whatever message they have for me." He hoped he was being convincingly reasonable even though he was more eager to see the pistol with every passing moment.

Sarah sighed but she really wasn't surprised. Michael was not one to let go of a problem until he had looked at it from every angle and done everything possible to resolve it. "Alright," she said, "but I'm going with you just to keep an eye on you."

"Me, too," insisted Isabel.

They decided to try the library first to satisfy Michael's urge to see the pistol. The pistols were owned by John Fairchild so it was thought that maybe they could provide a link to him somehow. Michael was happy that both Sarah and Isabel would be there with him. They also planned to visit the stables since one of the visions of John Fairchild had been reported to be seen there. Since John was the only ghost Michael had not yet encountered it might be interesting to see what message he might try to convey.

They entered the library led by Michael who went immediately to the pistol display. Sarah took in the room noticing the impressive collection of leather-bound books lining the shelves along the walls. Isabel kept a close eye on Michael. All three waited expectantly for several minutes.

Michael decided that he might be able to help things along by touching the pistol again. He picked the gun he remembered from earlier in the day, but to his surprise, nothing happened. He then tried the other, again without any sort of reaction. In fact, his obsessive urge to see and handle the pistols seemed to have evaporated. He looked around sheepishly, chuckled, and said, "Well, now I just feel silly."

"Maybe it's because we're here," speculated Sarah.

"I doubt it," replied Michael, "the very first time it happened was in a room full of people."

"I don't think we can force these things to happen on our schedule. I've never been one to believe in folks who claim they can summon spirits," offered Isabel, "I always think it is the spirits who are in control."

Now that Michael seemed to have broken from his obsession over the pistols Sarah, ever the librarian, felt free to peruse the shelves of the library. She was interested in what books might be found. The Fairchilds had quite the collection. She easily noted that the books were organized simply by author whether fiction or nonfiction. Thomas Paine's *Age of Reason* was tidily perched next to an assortment of works by Edgar Allan Poe. She pulled off the odd book or two to see if any first editions were to be found. Most of the books were in surprisingly good condition for being over 150 years old. She admired their leather bindings and goldleaf lettering. On a whim she walked over to where she thought she might find a copy of Charlotte Bronte's, *Jane Eyre*. This was her favorite book, she even had a paperback version with her, although opportunities to read it had been scarce. She thought it might be nice to revisit the story while away for the wedding. Her search was rewarded and she eagerly pulled the book from the shelves. She leafed through its beginning pages wanting to see if it was a first edition and stopped at a small slip of folded paper that had adhered to the inside cover. Interested, she removed it carefully. The paper was fragile but unfolded easily and did not threaten to break apart at the folds. The handwriting was tiny, as if to make the most of the small square of paper. The style was elegant compared to what passed for writing by today's standards.

Sarah read its contents aloud:

MY DEAREST LYDIA,

My sadness cannot be described. Although I long to ask for your hand, it is certain that your father will never bless our union. I do not want to come between a loving father and his beloved daughter. I now wish I had chosen to fight for the South against my own father's wishes, for I would rather have lost the war than my chance to share your love. Please meet me this evening at the stables. I could not bear to part from you without saying my farewells in person.

All my love, James W.

SARAH HANDED THE NOTE to Isabel knowing she would want to inspect it more closely.

Isabel took the note without comment but obviously lost in thought.

"Well, what do you make of it?" asked Michael after a few moments.

"I can't think how I could have missed this," replied Isabel, "I'm sure I've searched *every* book, many more than once."

"Well, it was a bit stuck to the page," said Sarah helpfully.

"Maybe, but I have spent a lot of time over the years searching for letters, journals, any primary sources of information about the Fairchild family and the plantation. I know that Bibles often have a place to record family events so I've concentrated my search focusing on the Bibles and prayer books. I guess I should have broadened my focus."

"Could someone have placed the letter in the book more recently?" asked Michael.

"Who?" asked Sarah.

"Gee, I don't know," admitted Michael, "maybe someone who didn't see it as a 'primary source' and just stuck it in the nearest book."

"No, I don't think so," said Isabel, answering Michael's question, "not the way it was stuck to the cover. It's been there for a while."

"Maybe the book itself wasn't in the library while you were searching. Perhaps it was shelved later. Are guests permitted access to the books?" Sarah questioned.

"There's no rule against guests entering the library, but I can't remember anyone ever asking to borrow one of its books," said Isabel.

"That's surprising," said Sarah sadly, "it's a wonderful collection."

Isabel and Michael shared a smile.

"Well, it is limited to books published before 1880. The books were found in all parts of the estate. I made it a project to collect and assemble them in this room. It was originally Thomas Fairchild's study; we began calling it the library after my project was completed. I think only historians and librarians would fully appreciate what it has to offer."

"I see," said Sarah, disappointed. She often complained that technology had replaced actual books with ebooks, audiobooks, internet blogs, and podcasts. She still liked the feel of a book in her hands and she loved to lose herself in a good book.

Sarah and Michael left the letter with Isabel and decided to walk up to the stables on their own. Isabel had some phone calls to make and she wanted to check with the chef to be sure he had everything he needed for the rehearsal dinner and reception.

Chapter 16

The summer day was hot and humid but there was enough shade to keep them comfortable on the walk up to the stables. As expected, the view from the hill was impressive and for a few minutes they remembered they were on vacation and took the time to enjoy the beautiful countryside. Michael noted that it was possible to make out part of the lake from this vantage point.

"I wonder where the dogs are, Isabel said they were trained to stay in this area," said Michael. As if on cue a friendly Australian shepherd ambled out to make their acquaintance.

They passed a few happy moments petting their new, furry friend when they heard movements coming from inside the stables. It sounded like a small scuffle and some giggles followed by a stern, Shhh! Michael and Sarah exchanged a look. There was something going on inside and neither of them supposed it was caused by ghosts. They went inside the stable in time to see a young woman grab her shoes and run out the opposite end. Sarah didn't see her face but her long, curly, distinctive red hair identified her as Joanna, Lynda's maid of honor. She wondered who she was here with. Whoever it was, he or she must have gotten out first because a quick search of the stables revealed no one.

"Well, what do you make of that?!" said Michael, "I thought that only happened in the movies." He was amused until he saw the look on Sarah's face.

"That - was Joanna," said Sarah indignantly, "I've been wondering why Lynda has been so neglected by her chosen maid of so-called honor!"

"Geez," said Michael "are you sure?"

Sarah scoffed, "Of course I am; didn't you see her hair?"

Of course Michael had seen her hair, but it had not made much of an impression on him. He attempted to convey the sense that "Oh yes, of course, now I see", but Sarah easily recognized his bluff and laughed.

They saw five horses housed in the stables and paid a visit to each one. They were gentle and seemed to enjoy a nice ear scratching. Sarah wished she had a treat to offer, but the horses didn't seem to mind the lack. Michael was attempting to whinny and snort like a horse with some success, at least the horse seemed to like it, answering back to him. They continued their "conversation" back and forth for a few minutes.

Hating to interrupt his fun Sarah asked, "Would you mind trying to remember more about your dream?"

Michael took a deep breath as if he was clearing his mind. "Let's see, I remember a woman with a cup of tea. I heard the sound of the spoon hitting the cup first. She was older, not old, just older, and I noticed her eyes, they were pretty, like yours, kind of green and brown."

"Hazel," interjected Sarah.

"Oh, okay, hazel."

"Go on," said Sarah, "sorry to interrupt."

"She was worried, I think. I also heard a dog barking every so often. He has to be the dog I've seen, the yellow lab, but I can't be sure; I only heard him barking in the dream."

"So this woman wasn't Lydia because she was too old. I'm guessing she was her mother...?" offered Sarah.

"No, her mother died in childbirth, it couldn't have been her. She was probably the aunt. Isabel said an aunt came to raise the children after the mother died. I remember something else, too. I saw a young woman opening a folded piece of paper and looking sad."

"Like the note we just found?"

"Yeah, now that you mention it," said Michael

"Anything else?" asked Sarah.

"No, it seems like there was more, but that's all I can think of."

"Well, I guess we should be getting back. What shall we do for dinner tonight?"

"How about we get the car and see what's in the area?" suggested Michael adding "After all, I've only had visions on the estate, might be nice to get away for a while."

"You need a get-away from your get-away? Wonderful," Sarah deadpanned.

Chapter 17

Isabel was satisfied with the preparations for the rehearsal dinner. The chef had assured her that he had enough food even with the additional guests, although he did make a point to Isabel that such a situation should not have been tolerated. The only wrinkle she had identified was a problem with the flower arrangements which she was able to resolve with a phone call. Two members of the wait staff had left messages that they would not be able to work the reception so she was looking for the employee roster to call in some replacements. She hoped she wouldn't have to pay any overtime.

A quick check of her emails, a brief phone call with a waiter who would be happy to work the reception, and a review of her to-do list brought her to the end of her work day. At last she could turn her thoughts to the situation with Mr. Daniels. Most concerning to her was the note found in the book. *How could I have missed that note?* She also wondered about the locket; she had stated that it would be hard to confirm that it belonged to the estate, however she believed Michael when he said it was discovered by the mysterious dog he had been seeing.

Mr. Daniels himself, was an enigma. With no previous experience of the kind he was having since his arrival, he was amazingly calm. She remembered other guests who had packed their bags and left after a single encounter. Mr. Daniels seemed to be taking it all in stride, at least until his behavior over the pistol. That, and his wife's reaction to it, were worrisome.

Isabel unfolded the note to read it again. It was signed James W. and he was a Union soldier. This was actual documentation of her presumption that Lydia had a secret beau. She was excited by the find yet frustrated by the fact that it had just conveniently appeared out of nowhere. She started to fold it up to take home, then unfolded it and went to her copier instead. Happy that there were no scheduled activities with the wedding party for the evening she left the original note on her desk and picked up her briefcase. She added the copy to a file she was taking home. Opening the bottom file drawer of the cabinet next to her desk she pulled out a large leather-bound book. She tucked it and the file inside her briefcase, grabbed her handbag and left her office.

Before heading downstairs she had a thought and stopped in the library. She wanted to take another look at the copy of *Jane Eyre*. If she was remembering correctly, it had been a favorite book of Lydia's. She planned to scan Lydia's letters to see if she could find where it was mentioned. She popped the volume into her briefcase and headed for home.

Chapter 18

Michael and Sarah waited at the carriage house for their car. They had a list of recommendations from Phoebe and planned to dine at a local eatery called The Sawmill Diner for a taste of authentic Southern cuisine. They tipped the valet and settled themselves into the car. During the winding, scenic drive into a small town called, Helen, they allowed themselves to slip back into a companionable silence for a time. The hills were a mosaic of greens and the sunset painted lovely pinks and oranges in the sky above them. They remarked that they couldn't have timed the drive better if they had planned it.

Unfortunately, the Sawmill Diner was closed for renovations so they settled for a little mom and pop pizza place called Joe's and ordered a mushroom pizza with extra cheese which was surprisingly satisfying.

Michael was happy to have some time alone with Sarah without fear of seeing the arrival of an upset bride. Sarah was just happy to see Michael acting more like his usual easy-going self. They chatted for a while about the food and the excellent service, what Michael called, "normal things", before the conversation returned to the ghosts of the estate. Sarah suggested asking Isabel if they could look at her collection of photos. She thought they might reveal a clue that Michael would notice given his recent experiences. Michael assured her that Isabel had already offered to share her notes with him, so the photos should be no problem.

"So, let's go back to the first time you saw the girl, you said you felt despair, right?"

"Yes," confirmed Michael.

"Then with the soldier you said you couldn't move, but you felt disbelief, shock, fear and rage."

"Uh huh," confirmed Michael in between bites of his slice, "I'm not sure I follow."

"I'm just thinking out loud," mused Sarah. "In your visits with Josiah, is there an overwhelming emotion?"

"No, not at all, we just talked."

"Yeah, I'm not sure how I feel about that," said Sarah, before asking, "How about in your dream? Did you feel anything strongly?"

"No, I was more of an observer then. The dream kept changing from one scene to another. My emotions were sort of neutral the whole time."

"Let's go back to the library vision with the soldier. Don't you think it's a little odd to feel disbelief, shock, fear and rage all at the same time? That's an awful lot of emotion for *one* person."

"I don't know," countered Michael, "rage can make you act rashly and those actions might cause you to feel disbelief or shock."

"Where does fear fit in?" asked Sarah

"Well, fear of the repercussions of your actions maybe ..."

"Is that how it felt to you? It seems like fear of repercussions might take a little time to kick in," offered Sarah.

Michael thought for a moment. "I was feeling them all at once, all at the same time."

"Where were you in the room? Do you remember?"

"I was near the desk by the pistol display case."

"Where was the soldier?"

"On the opposite side of the room near the fire," replied Michael.

"Interesting."

"Interesting? How?" asked Michael.

"Maybe there were *two* ghosts in the room, but you only saw one of them. Someone did the shooting; the soldier didn't shoot himself."

Michael put down what was his third slice of pizza. "When I finally broke free of the vision, or whatever it was, I was pointing the pistol which surprised me. Do you think I was the shooter?"

"Not you exactly, but maybe you were possessed by the ghost of the shooter?" theorized Sarah.

"Shit." Michael wasn't sure he was up for possession; he was a man who liked to feel in control of things.

"It kind of makes sense though," insisted Sarah, "You were positioned across the room from the soldier and later noticed that you were pointing the pistol. It also explains the wide range of emotions. Perhaps the soldier didn't really believe the person would actually shoot him so the disbelief and shock make sense. And anyone who has been shot would surely be fearful. If the shooter was Lydia's father, his rage makes sense, and maybe even shock at the result of his actions." She paused here for a moment before another thought occurred to her. "Does Isabel know where the soldier was shot, if it was in the library?"

Michael was now mentally adding possession to the list of visits, visions, and dreams. He didn't like the way the list was trending. When he finally registered her question he replied, "I don't know, she said there were few details about the shooting in the article she has. We can ask her though."

"Yes, let's do," said Sarah as she refilled her beer from the pitcher on the table, "we can also ask her opinion of my theory about your experience in the library. Did we set a time to meet with Isabel tomorrow?"

"No, I wish we had," said Michael. "I guess we'll just have to stop in and see if she has some time for us."

Chapter 19

Isabel sat on the couch in her living room leafing through her leather-bound record of sightings at the estate. The coffee table was strewn with old newspaper articles, photocopies of letters and photographs. She had already confirmed that the two sightings of the ghost she thought was John Fairchild had occurred in the third week of July. Both sightings were over five years ago so it appeared that Colonel Fairchild had been quiet in recent years, at least until now, during another third week of July.

She reread the article about the shooting which was dated Monday, July 17, 1865:

A SHOOTING WAS REPORTED on the estate of Colonel John Fairchild last week. Colonel Fairchild stated that a Yankee soldier was trespassing on his land. He stated that the young man would not heed his instructions to remove himself from the property. After several warnings he felt he had no choice but to take action. The trespasser was not able to be identified; his remains will be interred locally. Colonel Fairchild served valiantly with the First Confederate Infantry during the War for Southern Independence.

DEARLY BELOVED

ISABEL SHOOK HER HEAD at the dearth of information provided. There was no byline; it was buried at the bottom of page 4 as if the newspaper was going through the motions of recording that a death had occurred. This article would flunk a course of Journalism 101. Who? *An **unidentified** union soldier.* What? *A shooting.* Where? *Somewhere on Colonel Fairchild's land.* When? *Last week.* Why? *He was trespassing.* The lack of information and veracity of Colonel Fairchild was apparently accepted by whoever submitted the article. Isabel was sure that additional information had been known, but not reported. For example, no reason is given for the fact that the trespasser is identified as a Yankee soldier nearly three months after the formal end of the war. Was he still wearing a uniform? She made a note to ask Michael for more details from his vision in the library.

She stood to get a refill for her tea and accidentally knocked her pocket calendar onto the floor. Sighing, she bent to pick it up thinking how good it would be to see the back of Keith Stokes in just two more days. She opened the calendar to look ahead at her list of tasks for Thursday, July 21. Reassured that she had the day laid out and planned she headed to the kitchen, then stopped and picked up the calendar again. An illusive, yet nagging thought was trying to emerge. It just wouldn't surface. At last, she gave up the effort and focused on her tea. While the kettle heated, she tidied up the kitchen adding a few odd items to the dishwasher. Perhaps a pot of tea using her loose-leaf Darjeeling instead of a single use teabag might be the ticket and maybe even a few butter cookies. It wasn't long before her focus blurred as she carried out familiar tasks and her thoughts returned to the calendar.

Comfortably settled on the couch with her teapot steeping she picked up Lydia Fairchild's obituary. The newspaper was dated Monday, July 31, 1865.

LYDIA VICTORIA FAIRCHILD, aged 19, passed away last week after a brief illness. Lydia was the youngest daughter of Colonel John Smythe Fairchild of the Southern Oak Plantation. She is survived by her father and three older brothers, Thomas Joseph Fairchild, Robert Henry Fairchild and George Frederick Fairchild. She was preceded in death by her mother, Virginia Stanton Fairchild and two brothers William Paul Fairchild and John Smyth Fairchild, Jr. who were lost in the War for Southern Independence. A private funeral was held and internment took place on the Fairchild Estate.

AGAIN, ISABEL NOTED the lack of details. The illness was unspecified and no date of death reported. A private funeral was unusual for the Fairchild Family. The article regarding the death of her mother was top of the fold on the society page and included lists of dignitaries in attendance, descriptions of notable flower arrangements, and quotes from several attendees. This appeared to be another occurrence that John Fairchild wanted to pass without a lot of attention. Given John Fairchild's noted affection for his daughter, Isabel wondered why no one questioned the lack of a formal public send-off for a beloved family member. She made a note to check subsequent editions of the Recorder's society pages to see if any mention may have been made in the weeks after the funeral.

Like an itch she couldn't scratch she felt she was missing something obvious. An idea finally floated to the surface. She picked up her pocket calendar and checked the page for July. This past Monday was the 17th, next Monday was the 24^{h}. The article about the shooting was from the Recorder was dated Monday, July 17. She then compared calendars for 1865 and the current year. They were identical. Interesting, but was it important? She decided it was merely interesting but was pleased to note that the discovery seemed to satisfy her illusive itch.

The thing that was troubling her most of all was the note Sarah found in the copy of *Jane Eyre* in the library. There was just no way to authenticate it. If only James had signed his full name, she could attempt to find another sample of his handwriting to compare. She wished it had been dated. She wondered, not for the first time, how it had come to be where it was and how she had missed it in all of her research. There were simply too many unanswered questions and little likelihood of answering them before the end of the Mr. Daniel's stay.

She poured herself a cup of tea and pulled out the copy *Jane Eyre* to examine it more closely. It was an elegant book, deep brown leather with gilded top pages. The binding was sagging a bit but the pages were securely sewn in. The story was familiar to her more from a movie version than the novel itself which she had read as a girl. She smiled and wondered what Sarah would have to say about that.

She was astonished to see yet another small square of paper tucked in the pages and gently tugged it free. It had writing on it in Lydia's hand:

Mrs. James Alden Ward
Mrs. Lydia Victoria Ward
Lydia Ward
Lydia and James

ISABEL STARED AT THE page in front of her. She knew at once what it was. Lydia's fantasy played out on the tiny piece of paper before her. She felt a twinge of sympathy and sadness for dreams that were never realized for this young woman. How childlike to try out names to see how they fit, like trying on a new outfit. She imagined, not for the first time, Lydia dying of a broken heart.

Chapter 20

Michael and Sarah arrived back at the carriage house to return their car. They were walking toward their cottage when Michael remembered that he left his cell phone behind. He told Sarah to go on ahead; it would take time for the valet to bring the car back around so he could retrieve it. Since there was no one in the carriage house he decided to try to walk up to where the cars were parked behind the main house, maybe he could meet the valet halfway. This proved to be a good idea and soon he had his phone and was walking downhill toward the carriage house.

His eyes caught the silhouette of someone standing near the gardens. It was late, nearly midnight and he didn't expect to see anyone out walking at this late hour. He came to the junction of two paths, one leading toward the front of the mansion and the other toward the carriage house and guest cottages. Against his better judgement he walked toward the mansion. The size and the posture of the figure looked familiar.

"Hello, it's a lovely evening, isn't it?" greeted Michael.

"Yassuh," returned Josiah.

Michael took a breath. *Who better to ask?*

"I sure do have a lot of questions," he said.

"Ah magine so," said Josiah.

"Can you answer them?"

"Mebbe."

"Well, is there anything you want to tell me?"

"They's rules. You hasta ask me questions, suh."

"I see. I have so many, I don't know where to start."

"Best start somewhere, times a wastin'," advised Josiah.

"Of course. Do you know how Lydia died?"

Josiah hesitated before answering, "Yes suh."

"Was she sick?"

"No suh."

"No? I thought she died of an illness. Was it an accident?"

"It wuz and an' it wuzn't. Folks roun' heah was all worked up," said Josiah.

"What were they worked up about?" asked Michael.

"Master Fairchile didn't want no Yankee boy neah his lil' girl. He wuzn't havin' none of it. Miss Lyddie been seein' that boy by the stables for weeks afore he even knowed. I knowed it, I tole her no good come of it. He tole her, too, but she was foolish and spoilt and headstrong."

"Who else told her?" asked Michael.

"Mista James tole her, he tole she was hurtin' her daddy. He say he was fixin' to leave but she begged him to stay," Josiah looked heartbroken at the memory.

"What happened?" asked Michael.

"They's rules and I already done broke 'em" said Josiah miserably.

Michael could see that Josiah was getting more distressed with each question. He decided to go in a different direction.

"Josiah, do you know what's been happening to me?" he asked.

"I knows you ain't seein' things aright. You jus' see a part of it. They's more."

"Do you know anything about the locket at the lake?"

"That was a terrible thing the way her daddy tore it from her neck. Said she wuzn't to take no tokens from that Yankee boy."

Suddenly, Josiah looked wary. He took a step back into the shadows and was gone. For the first time Michael saw him disappear; it reminded him of watching Sarah disappear from the sitting room during the Welcome Dinner party. He walked briskly back toward the Magnolia Cottage.

Chapter 21

Staff who worked nights at Southern Oak occasionally had their own stories to tell. If room service was requested by guests in the cottages after dark it was delivered by two members of the wait staff. The sounds of the night: crickets, owls, coyotes, even the wind in the trees could stir the imagination in directions one should not go. Even worse was when the quiet took over; when even a cricket declined to chirp. It was an unnatural silence and one to be avoided.

Jonah did not mind working nights, usually the tips were good and the interruptions few. He'd even been able to sneak in forty winks on occasion. Nights in July, however, were a different story; it was hard to find anyone who wanted to work then. This year staff who agreed to work nights during July were offered time and a half. Jonah couldn't turn down that kind of money so he decided to roll the dice.

He was scrolling through Instagram on his phone and jumped when the desk phone rang.

"Southern Oak, you've reached the carriage house. This is Jonah speaking, how may I help you?" He listened to the request from the guest before replying. "Yes suh, I'll get that to you as soon as possible."

"Damn."

"What is it?" asked his co-worker for the evening, Cindy. Cindy was a new hire who just plain didn't know any better than to agree to overnight hours.

"Dogwood Cottage is allergic to feather pillows. They need foam." He sounded as though he thought they were making it up just to make him jump through hoops.

"So, take them some foam pillows, what's the big deal?" asked Cindy.

"Not me," corrected Jonah, "we".

"Why? Need help carrying pillows? I'm sure you can manage it."

"The rule is that two employees have to go at night. So, me and you."

"Who will answer the phone?"

"I'll forward the calls to the main house," replied Jonah with a shrug.

"This is silly, you can handle it by yourself," insisted Cindy.

"Nope, it's both of us, or I'll report you. I'm not going out there alone. There's a reason for the rule," he added ominously.

"Are you serious?" asked his co-worker.

"Dogwood is the farthest cottage from here. We'll take the cart."

Soon Jonah, Cindy and four foam pillows – because Jonah wanted to be sure not to have to make two trips – were piled onto the golf cart. Jonah also had two flashlights and a supply of anything else that might be asked for at the last minute: towels, soap, shampoo, lotion, and even coffee packets.

The night was cool and there was a small breeze. Jonah stayed on the well-lit path and Cindy held on to the framework of the cart in lieu of a seatbelt of any kind. She wished he would go a little slower. She did remember the bit about two employees on nighttime errands from her orientation, but figured it wouldn't be enforced. She was miffed that Jonah was being such a stickler for the rules.

Once they were away from the carriage house Cindy admitted to herself that she understood why Jonah wanted someone with him. The only light was from the path, beyond it was almost pitch black. A waxing crescent moon did little to illuminate the night sky. The cottages were not clustered together but quite a distance apart along the winding gravel road. She peered through the night looking for the next house. The Pine Cottage was dark, everyone must be in bed, content with their feather pillows. There were some lights on in the White Oak Cottage. It was a relief to see their warm glow and imagine happy vacationers inside.

They continued on silently, neither one wanting to put voice to their dread. At last they arrived at the Dogwood Cottage. Jonah applied the brake, grabbed the pillows and hopped out of the cart. He wasn't surprised to see Cindy at his side.

"Now you see why we don't go out alone?" he asked.

"Oh let's just get this over with," replied Cindy. She was looking forward to seeing the guests, even for just a moment.

Jonah smiled, happy he had made his point. The guests were grateful for the new pillows and accepted all four gladly. When Jonah asked if there was anything else they needed they declined and wished them a goodnight complete with a very generous tip. For the first time Jonah thought maybe he should have gone alone; now he would have to split the tip.

"This place is creepy at night," allowed Cindy who was also pleased with the size of the tip and happy she had at last agreed to come along.

"I know, but usually the requests are for room service and those are handled by the main house staff, so we don't get many calls. Also the pay is good," said Jonah.

"Why is time and a half offered only for nights in July?" asked Cindy. "Seems like it should be for all summer at least."

"That would cost them too much, especially since we mostly just sit around trying to stay awake," said Jonah avoiding a direct response. He mostly tried to ignore the reputation of Southern Oak being haunted.

They were approaching the Magnolia Cottage, the last cottage before the carriage house, when Jonah noted the unnatural silence. The hairs on the back of his neck stood up and he was instantly on guard. He glanced over at Cindy who also looked apprehensive. As they drew nearer the cottage Jonah thought he saw several shadowy figures hovering near every window of the cottage. Jonah slowed the golf cart to peer into the darkness. The light bathing the pathway made it difficult to see anything beyond clearly. The shadows appeared to note their passage pulling away from the windows, then they seemed to come together in a mass of darkness.

"Don't slow down," urged Cindy, "Go, *go!*"

As the cluster of shadows rushed after them, Jonah sped away as fast as the cart would go. Cindy twisted her body around to see them hurtling toward them.

"What is that?!" she cried.

Jonah didn't answer since he had no answer to give. He just kept driving until he saw the welcome sight of the carriage house driveway. They both bolted from the cart and rushed inside locking the door behind them.

Jonah was shaking as he picked up the phone and punched a series of numbers.

Chapter 22

Isabel had finally turned in for the night just a little past midnight. She had stayed up too late, she knew, and would regret it in the morning. She was excited to share her discoveries with Mr. Daniels. In addition to the small square of paper found in *Jane Eyre*, there was a photograph of Lydia in which she appeared to be wearing a heart-shaped locket. She was eager to compare it with the one from the lake.

They had not arranged a time to meet which was a pity; she really should have seen to that. She was about to get out of bed to check her calendar for tomorrow when she changed her mind and settled into a comfortable sleeping position instead. It would have to wait until the morning.

She was enjoying that lovely pleasantly sleepy feeling but not yet asleep when the phone rang on her nightstand. She really should get rid of her landline she thought grumpily. *This can't be good* she told herself.

"Hello," she answered and waited.

"Ms. Pennington, this is Jonah. I'm working tonight at the carriage house and we just had a request from the Dogwood Cottage. On our way back we saw something very strange at the Magnolia Cottage. I thought you would want to know. Mr. Daniels and his wife are in Magnolia."

Isabel listened carefully. She noted Jonah's use of "we" and "our" pleased that it seemed that the rules were being observed. At the mention of Magnolia Cottage and Mr. Daniels she sat up, no longer sleepy. She took a moment to consider the situation. It was late, too late to make a courtesy call, if all was well it would only disturb their evening.

"Ms. Pennington?" Since there had been no reply Jonah checked to see if she was still on the line.

"Yes, Jonah, I heard you. Do our guests appear to have been disturbed? Have you heard anything from them?" she asked.

"No ma'am, well, at least I don't think so. We didn't stick around to find out. They haven't called."

"What do you think you saw?"

"There were like shadows at all the windows. We didn't see them on our way out, only when we came back. They seemed to know we were there and chased us all the way back to the carriage house," said Jonah.

"Who are you working with tonight, Jonah?"

"The new girl, Cindy."

"Is she okay?"

"Cindy, are you okay?" Jonah didn't know so he decided to ask her directly.

Isabel heard someone murmur something in the background.

"She says she's okay but she won't go back out there again and she doesn't care if you fire her. Uh, I don't want to go back out either, truth be told," said Jonah.

"Very well, if you get any more requests, refer them to the Main House. I'll call the Main House to let them know. But Jonah, if you hear from the Daniels, call me right away. If they show up at the carriage house, let them inside."

"Yes ma'am," said Jonah.

"When does your shift end?"

"We get off at seven. I'm also on tomorrow from 4 to 11 for the rehearsal dinner," said Jonah.

"I'd like to see you tomorrow after you sign in to work, please. And what about Cindy? Does she work tomorrow?" She waited for Jonah to relay her question and was surprised when the next voice was Cindy.

"Ms. Pennington, this is Cindy and I can speak for myself. I get off at seven and I don't work again until Saturday for the wedding reception. I'm part-time, just for the summer."

"I see," said Isabel, "Then you have a little time to decide whether you'd like to continue with us at Southern Oak or not. You see it is important that you not share your experience with our guests. If you feel you cannot keep this confidential, we will have to let you go. Please don't make up your mind just yet, but I'll need to know by Sunday morning if you cannot work the wedding. I'm very sorry this happened to you."

The conversation ended. Isabel made a quick call to the Main House before settling back under the covers, impossibly tired. She got the feeling that Cindy would be willing to tough it out for the summer and Jonah knew the drill; he was solid. She really didn't want to be hiring replacements half-way through the summer months.

Chapter 23

Michael had already enjoyed another slice of cold pizza from the box they took home from Joe's. Sarah did not know how he could eat it cold, but he claimed to prefer it that way. She was sitting up in bed with a cup of decaf on the nightstand and her copy of *Jane Eyre* open in front of her.

"What's that story about anyway? I know it's supposed to be a classic," asked Michael.

"Basically, a young governess falls in love with her employer and eventually he asks her to marry him. At the wedding someone objects and reveals that her employer, Mr. Rochester, is already married."

"Uh oh," interjected Michael.

"Uh huh, it's tragic because his wife is insane and locked up in the attic. Eventually everything works out when his crazy wife kills herself and burns down the house. Jane and Rochester get to live happily ever after. The end." Sarah made an effort to keep the summary short and sweet, since she knew Michael was a wait-for-the-movie kind of guy.

"No happy ending for wife number one or the house," pointed out Michael.

Sarah chuckled, "Nope, a tragic ending for the crazy wife."

"Interesting that the narrative includes a wedding with an objection from an attendee," pointed out Michael.

"I hadn't thought of that," said Sarah, amused.

"So, are you going to read for a while?"

"Hmm, can you think of another way to occupy ourselves?"

"I can," said Michael and slid into bed beside Sarah who happily abandoned her book.

Michael had left the light on in the bathroom, but the main room was unlit. That made the lights of a vehicle as it sped past their cottage more noticeable.

"That's odd," said Michael sitting up.

"Only because we're getting used to the absence of traffic. I wonder what it was; it seemed to be going faster than it should," observed Sarah.

"Phoebe said all cars are kept in the valet parking area," remembered Michael.

"Probably employees then," reasoned Sarah.

"I guess so," said Michael as he settled himself back into bed.

A few minutes later Michael was forced to interrupt his tender ministrations to his wife when he suddenly felt very uneasy. He shuddered and sat back up, wary. Sarah felt it, too, and held his arm looking for reassurance.

"Get dressed and put your shoes on," he whispered as he climbed out of bed looking for his own shoes.

Sarah reached for her robe, shoes on her feet and drew closer to Michael.

"What is it?" she was still whispering.

"No idea, but I don't like it. It feels wrong," Michael said softly.

"I feel it, too, it's oppressive, and not in a hot-summer-day sort of way," said Sarah.

They both stood at the ready, not sure what they were preparing for. Michael peered out the window near his side of the bed, but all he saw was blackness; he couldn't even make out the shrubbery he knew was there.

"I can't see a damn thing. Isn't there a moon tonight?" he asked.

"I wasn't noticing," said Sarah.

Moments later, still standing at the ready, they were relieved when lights of the returning vehicle broke through the curtain of black and the putter of a motor pierced the eerie quiet that had descended. The gloom disappeared as quickly as it had arrived.

"What the hell ...?" said Sarah.

"Exactly," replied Michael.

Chapter 24

FRIDAY

Friday morning was a busy one for Isabel. She had overslept and began her day on the run. Her first stop, even before going up to her office, was the Grand Ballroom to see that it was being set up according to her instructions. Then it was on to the Main Hall to see if the canopy had been delivered and was in place. Florists would arrive later in the day to adorn it for the ceremony. After making sure everything was in place for the rehearsal that evening, she turned her attention to the dinner that would follow. She stopped in at the kitchen to chat with the catering manager and beg a cup of coffee. She finally made it to her office a little after nine.

Seated at her desk she took a moment to enjoy that first sip of coffee. At heart a tea drinker, she nevertheless required a bracing cup of coffee to begin her day. She looked at her emails shooting off quick replies between sips of the eye-opening brew.

Since the rehearsal dinner was to be a buffet, she felt they were adequately staffed, but she still wanted to have one more server for the wedding reception. She had a few calls out and hoped she would hear from someone today. Cindy was still a question mark; she hoped her hunch would prove correct and she would not have to find a replacement for her as well.

Her first phone call of the day was to the Magnolia Cottage. She was pleased when Michael answered after the third ring.

"Good morning, Mr. Daniels," she said more brightly than she felt, "how is your morning coming along?" She waited anxiously to hear how he would respond; it might tell her if they had been troubled by Jonah's shadows.

"Call me Michael," he reminded her, "I'm glad you called, I know you must be busy, but we did hope to meet with you again today."

"That's the reason for my call, I know it's short notice, but, is now a good time for you? I am expecting to hear from the florists and musicians later in the day so this is the best time for me," she explained. She was very happy that he seemed neither angry or upset.

"I'm on vacation so my morning is wide open; Sarah and I will be right up," said Michael.

"Perfect!" said Isabel. "Just one more thing, would you bring along the necklace you found by the lake?"

"Happy to," said Michael, "we'll see you in five."

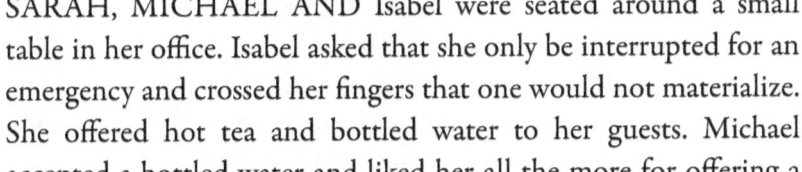

SARAH, MICHAEL AND Isabel were seated around a small table in her office. Isabel asked that she only be interrupted for an emergency and crossed her fingers that one would not materialize. She offered hot tea and bottled water to her guests. Michael accepted a bottled water and liked her all the more for offering a sensible alternative to sweetened iced tea.

"Where shall we start?" she asked thinking that her discoveries could wait until she was sure they had passed an uneventful night.

Sarah and Michael exchanged a look, seeming to make up their minds. Sarah spoke first.

"Michael had another of his unusual experiences last night and this time I got to go along for the ride," she said.

Crap thought Isabel before saying aloud, "Oh dear, I was hoping that Jonah was overreacting." She decided not to feign ignorance of the event.

"Jonah?" asked Sarah surprised.

"Jonah was on duty last night. He gave me a call at home."

"Interesting," said Michael, "what did he say?"

"He was taking pillows to some guests and used the golf cart to deliver them. On his way back he saw some unusual shadows near your cottage. He seemed to feel that they chased him back to the carriage house," she tried to be as brief as possible, no need to embellish. She waited with interest for his response.

"Well, that explains the lights at least," said Michael to Sarah who nodded in agreement.

"It was really only a few minutes," added Sarah, "but a very weird and frightening few minutes."

"Yes," said Michael, "I was unnerved and on guard without any apparent reason for it."

"Yet you didn't call for help," observed Isabel.

"Who would we call?" asked Sarah.

Michael grinned at the perfect set up, "Ghostbusters?" Both Sarah and Isabel chuckled and shook their heads at the lame joke.

"But seriously," said Sarah, "we could scarcely dial 9-1-1 and report that we were afraid of the dark."

"No, I suppose not. So, where does this leave us?" asked Isabel. She didn't think they would ask to check out, but best not to assume.

"Confused and bewildered," said Michael, "but also curious and determined to stick it out, at least until check-out on Sunday."

"And, Sarah, are you in agreement?" Isabel took a lesson from her experience with Cindy the previous evening and addressed Sarah directly.

"I guess I can hang in here until 11 am Sunday," she agreed although not as heartily as Michael's assertion had been.

"We can leave at ten if you like, dear," offered her devoted husband.

Isabel was eager to see the locket again. Michael had it with him and it looked very much like the one in the photo Isabel had displayed on the table. The photo was one of Lydia sitting primly at the piano, her back to it. She wore a high neckline with a delicate lace collar. The front of her shoulder length hair was tied back with a ribbon making it easier to see the necklace. "I've only found three photos of Lydia: a group family photo, the one of her on the pony with Josiah, and this one," she revealed.

"You can't see it well enough to really compare, but how many silver heart-shaped lockets could one girl have?" pointed out Sarah.

Isabel believed that the photo supported the notion that the necklace had belonged to Lydia, but unfortunately, it would not be enough to confirm provenance definitively.

Next, she shared the slip of paper she had found in the pages of *Jane Eyre* with them.

Sarah smiled; she too, recognized that Lydia was experimenting with a dreamed of name change. It took an extra beat for Michael to make the connection.

"So, our soldier is James Alden Ward," he said at last.

"It would seem so. Now I will be able to do more exhaustive research on him. It would be exciting to be able to substantiate the widely held notion of the secret beau." She was obviously eager to learn more, but disappointed that she would not have time to visit the local library until after the wedding weekend.

Sarah looked with interest at the display of material Isabel had collected on the Fairchild Family. She picked up a stack of letters, glancing at Isabel, as if to ask permission.

"May I?" she asked.

"Of course," Isabel nodded, "the stack you are holding are Lydia's letters. Most of them were written to her father while he was away during the war years. A few were written to her Aunt Katherine. It seems she had to leave the estate for a few months at the death of her brother; she and Lydia exchanged a couple of letters during that time."

Sarah began to thumb through the letters selecting one to open.

"Michael," said Isabel remembering to call him by his first name, "May I ask you more about your vision in the study? Can you tell me more about the soldier?"

Michael thought for a moment before answering. "He was young, he didn't speak. No one ever speaks in my visions. He looked horrified and as if he was screaming."

"What do you remember about his clothes?"

"Uh, not a lot. He had on blue plants and a blood-stained woven shirt of some kind. They looked too big for him, he seemed emaciated."

"What made you believe him to be a soldier?" asked Isabel.

"Oh!" said Michael understanding what she was getting at. "It was his cap, he was holding what looked to be a military cap."

"I see," said Isabel satisfied with his answer, "it's called a kepi."

"Interesting, I didn't know that," said Michael.

"Sarah and I have been wondering if you know where the shooting of the soldier took place?" asked Michael.

"No, it's a question I've often asked myself. The article regarding the shooting only mentions that he was trespassing on the estate, it's nonspecific on the exact location. As I said, it's vague on many of the details."

"Michael, look at this!" exclaimed Sarah, "It's a letter Lydia wrote to her aunt. It seems she finally read a book that Aunt Katherine had given to her as a gift: *Jane Eyre!*"

"You're kidding, really?!" asked Michael, "That's one of Sarah's favorites, she even brought a copy with her," this last was directed at Isabel who looked a little confused that Sarah should be so enthused that Lydia enjoyed a book.

"She thanked her aunt for recommending it, said she loved it, planned to reread it and would cherish it always," finished Sarah offering the letter to Isabel.

Isabel took the letter and quickly scanned its contents.

"It does sound like it was a favorite of hers," agreed Isabel adding, "the sort of book where one may tuck a special memento inside. I do remember reading this letter, but didn't see it as anything particularly note-worthy at the time."

A quiet knock at the door interrupted their meeting. It was Katie, from Guest Services. She apologized saying that she hated to interrupt but she had an important message: for Sarah.

Chapter 25

Isabel was surprised when the interruption was *not* for her. Michael's reaction was mild irritation on Sarah's behalf. He was sure it was Lynda, once again placing her problems at Sarah's feet. Katie confirmed that Miss Fuller had been trying to find Mrs. Daniels and reached out to Guest Services as a last resort. Knowing that she was the bride made Katie feel that the interruption was merited. Isabel agreed, setting her mind at ease.

Once alone with Isabel, Michael asked what she thought about the shadows Jonah had reported. He had not wanted to ask this in front of Sarah so her absence was convenient in this respect. Isabel was thoughtful for a few moments before answering.

"I have shared with you a few of the experiences our guests have had over the years, but neglected to include anything about staff experiences," she said finally.

"I see," said Michael hoping there was more. "You did mention some of your experiences."

"Yes, but many on our staff have seen unusual things while working on the property. Enough that we have a rule about nighttime errands being made by two employees. Some members of our staff have seen faces reflected in windows, mirrors and even the lake. Others have heard the sounds of music, weeping, moaning, and even barking. Shadows and mists are frequently reported when outdoors. The vast majority of employee sightings are reported by those on the overnight shift. It just doesn't seem possible for so many on the staff to have psychic abilities. I think it more likely that they have simply disturbed our restless spirits in the performance of their duties."

"You said some have reported shadows and mists when outdoors, what about rain while indoors," asked Michael.

Isabel appeared to be taken aback by this question, "Why do you ask?"

"Because my visions in the sitting room and in the library, all had rain falling in the room. I could swear I was getting wet during the episode, but would be totally dry once it had ended," revealed Michael.

"Fascinating," said Isabel "I'm surprised you haven't mentioned this until now."

"I guess I've been more focused on the people and the feelings in the visions," said Michael.

"At the time of the shooting the region had been undergoing unusually severe downpours. It was during this time that the tree was uprooted from the saturated soil and damaged the house. I don't know which happened first, the shooting or the damage to the roof, but both occurred around the third week of July, 1865."

"Do you know if anyone in the house was hurt when the tree fell? Maybe Lydia was at the piano and got injured?" asked Michael.

"I don't think so, but I can't be sure. I know about the damage because John wrote about it in a letter to one of his sons in Atlanta. And there are receipts for some of the materials he needed to purchase for the repair that were found in his papers," said Isabel.

"So others have seen shadows," stated Michael returning to his earlier thought, "what do you think about them?"

"I haven't seen them myself, but I believe that the staff are seeing something that frightens them enough to report it to me. Unfortunately, some of them resign, but most stay on hoping it was a one-time thing, or else convinced that they simply let their imagination run away with them. My own experiences have centered around Josiah and the dog," replied Isabel.

"Have other members of the staff seen Josiah?" asked Michael.

"None who have reported it to me. Of course, sightings of Josiah are not what I would call frightening. I do include the staff sightings in my ledger if you'd like to see it," said Isabel helpfully.

"May I take it with me to my cottage? I think it's something Sarah might be interested in."

"Certainly."

"Speaking of Josiah, I saw him again last night. He was near the gardens where I saw him the first time we spoke. It was an unusual visit – for a visit with Josiah. I haven't told Sarah; I'm not sure why," he finished.

Isabel took a moment to appreciate how casually Michael could relate his interactions with Josiah. She perked up at his characterization of this particular visit as unusual.

"What did he say?" she wondered.

Michael was thoughtful. He didn't want to leave anything out.

"He basically confirmed that John Fairchild had discovered that Lydia was meeting the soldier secretly at the stables. He said John tore the necklace from Lydia's neck. It must have been a scene. I asked him if he knew how Lydia died and he told me it wasn't an illness so your newspaper article didn't get their facts straight. Then he said something to the effect that my visions are incomplete. The most interesting thing to me was his answer to my question about whether her death was an accident: he said it was and it wasn't."

Isabel listened with interest. She was busily making notes on a pad of paper she had in front of her.

"So Josiah knows how she died, but wouldn't tell you straight out. I've often wondered if her beau's death might have driven her to take her own life. It would explain why her father would want to keep the details private."

"Yes," said Michael, "and I agree that my visions are probably missing pieces."

"You do?" asked Isabel.

"Sure, the first vision was just of an empty sitting room; the second added a piano and the girl making it more complete. In the study I just saw the soldier who had been shot, there had to be more that I didn't see."

"It seems like you are having two visions, one of the girl, and the other of the soldier," pointed out Isabel.

"Maybe," allowed Michael. "One more thing about Josiah; this visit felt a little different. When I began asking him questions it was as if we had both set aside any pretense that he was simply the gardener. He warned me that 'there are rules' about how he could answer me. His visits are always brief; this time he tried to hurry me along as if he could be pulled away at any moment. And, he seemed apprehensive and wary. For the first time he didn't wait until I turned away: he disappeared right in front of me."

"My word!" exclaimed Isabel. She was frankly surprised that the Daniels hadn't packed their bags and left by now. "This is fascinating. Seems like he really is trying to help. I just can't figure out if he's wanting to help you or Lydia."

"Why not both?" observed Michael.

"Perhaps you should have a few questions in mind in case you see him again, especially since his appearances are so brief," suggested Isabel.

Michael agreed, already beginning to formulate a question about Lydia's death being both accidental and not. They parted with Michael planning to search out Sarah and revisit the stables.

There was much to think about. It would be a challenge to focus on the tasks she had scheduled for the day. Isabel took a few minutes to get her notes organized before reluctantly returning to the work she was paid to do.

Chapter 26

Katie escorted Sarah to a bench in the hallway near Isabel's office where Lynda sat waiting, a moist tissue in her hands. Lynda looked up, evidence of dried tears on her face. Sarah sighed and stood next to her. *What has Keith done now?*

"Maybe you'd like to walk with me back to my cottage," she suggested. She was thinking on her feet and thought they would have more privacy in her cottage than Lynda's room in the Main House.

Lynda nodded and rose from her seat, her head held down as if it was too heavy to lift.

"Have you eaten anything?" asked Sarah not waiting for an answer before adding, "I'm hungry. How about we order something from room service? Then we'll have a nice chat."

They were almost to the door when Sarah saw Steve striding across the foyer toward them. He reminded her of Michael with his long legs making quick work of the distance between them. Sarah made an attempt to look as though she and Lynda were simply enjoying some time together, but Steve seemed to know that something was amiss.

Lynda stopped when she saw him.

"I didn't know you were here this morning," she told him in a soft voice.

"I came to bring Keith his shoes for the wedding, they gave him the wrong size. He wasn't in his room though so I left them with his parents." Steve could tell she was upset; he touched her shoulder, trying to make eye contact without success.

"I've had a huge fight with my dad," Lynda tried to stifle a sob without success. Eyes downcast, Lynda took a deep breath before adding, "Daddy got the addendum to the bill; he knew it was coming, but it was much more than he expected. He told Keith that he would not cover the deposit for the cancelled DJ, then called him irresponsible and self-centered. Keith stormed out and now I can't find him anywhere."

So much for privacy thought Sarah.

"What can I do to help?" asked Steve.

"Would you try to find Keith?" asked Sarah.

"I've already looked everywhere I can think of," said Lynda.

"Well, he has to be somewhere," said the always practical Sarah. "Did you look outside the Main House?"

"No, I tried his room, his parent's room and the sitting room. He was there with some friends earlier this morning. I also looked in the lounge; they serve drinks there," said Lynda.

"Maybe he took a walk to clear his head," suggested Sarah. "There's a very pretty view near the stables at the top of the rise. Or he might be by the lake."

"I'll try both," said Steve. "First, I'll ask the valet if they brought his car out for him. We'll figure this out, Lynda. I'll call you on your cell if I find him." He was gone before they even had time to thank him.

At the cottage Sarah offered Lynda the comfy seat with the hassock and grabbed the phone to order sandwiches. She filled a mug with water and a tea bag and popped it into the microwave.

Tending to these simple tasks gave her a chance to think and Lynda a few moments to regain her composure. She was relieved to see that Lynda seemed to relax noticeably in the unfamiliar surroundings.

When the second mug was announced by the beep of the microwave, Sarah finished preparing the tea and set both mugs on the coffee table. She settled herself on the couch near Lynda.

"So, where did all of this happen?" asked Sarah.

"In my room. Keith was there; we were going to go out for breakfast, but he'd come to say that something came up and he would have to cancel."

"Did he say what came up?" asked Sarah who had to remind herself to appear neutral.

"He didn't have time, that's when Daddy came in waving the envelope with the amended bill. Everything happened all at once."

"This may be none of my business," said Sarah, "but does the cost represent a hardship for your dad, or is he just upset with Keith as a matter of principle?"

"Oh, it's not really the money. My parents wanted to spend a lot more on a wedding at home. They couldn't impress as many friends and business associates at a destination wedding. They really wanted to put on a show. I wanted something smaller, more intimate; the only way I could see to do it was to leave town." Sarah had not known any of this. She felt badly for her friend who was obviously caught between two very strong personalities.

"What does your dad do for a living?" asked Sarah.

"He's in real estate. Have you heard of Fuller Real Estate Solutions?"

"Oh!" said Sarah, "I didn't know that was your dad! I guess he can afford a few extra guests."

"Yes, but they are not guests of his choosing, not the guests he wants to impress," said Lynda miserably. "I do get his point though, Keith's extra guests weren't even on the original guest list. We didn't send any of them an invitation."

This, too, was news to Sarah. Michael would call Keith "a piece of work".

"How did this get to be so out of control? Why would Keith do that?"

"I really don't know. I thought everything was set. I would never have thought Keith capable of some of the things he's done. We made the guest list together, we chose the music together, the menu, all of it."

Sarah decided on a change of topic she was curious about.

"I've been meaning to ask you about Joanna, how did you meet?"

"Joanna? We've been friends since 4th grade; she's outgoing and adventurous and always up for anything. She was always first on the dance floor, eager to jump in front of a karaoke microphone, and she'd do anything for attention. I always admired her willingness to look bad trying something new. I guess they say opposites attract; we're nothing alike."

"She sounds like she's a lot of fun," said Sarah smiling.

"She is. She helped me socialize and make friends. I was not much of a joiner in school and she made it easier. Being her friend had its challenges though. At school she got into more than her share of trouble. You know the kind of thing: skipping school, cheating on the occasional test, smoking in the girls' restroom. Nothing too terrible and she never did anything to get me in trouble."

"How come you've never mentioned her before?" asked Sarah.

"I haven't seen her since our senior year in college. She moved out-of-state after graduation, but we kept in touch. You know, social media posts and Christmas cards. In high school we promised to be each other's maid of honor like girls sometimes do. When she heard that I was engaged, she actually phoned which surprised me. She seemed to assume that she would be maid of honor and made me swear not to make her wear an ugly dress. I'm embarrassed to say that in spite of my promise, I hadn't planned to ask her, but then I thought, why not? Maybe it's time to reconnect."

"Did Joanna have lots of boyfriends?" asked Sarah.

"Oh yes! She was popular; she had guys lined up hoping for a date. Why do you ask?"

"Except for the manicures, I haven't seen much of her. Did she bring a plus one?"

"No, but that's never stopped her from having a good time," Lynda seemed to continue to consider Sarah's comment. "Oh, I see. You're wondering why she hasn't been more of a confidant considering all the trouble with Keith. She's just never been that kind of friend to me the way you have. And I never thought I'd need this kind of support." She paused as a thought was beginning to surface. "Sarah, I am *so* sorry; I've been imposing on your friendship."

"Oh no, not at all!" insisted Sarah, who winced inwardly remembering her grumblings over the situation. "I'm honored that you feel you can come to me. It's just natural to think that the maid of honor might also be someone you'd go to." Sarah knew she'd be feeling guilty about this conversation for some time. She was kicking herself for adding to Lynda's already very full plate of problems.

"What am I going to do?" asked Lynda unhappily.

"You need to talk to Keith, hear his thoughts," said Sarah. *If he has any.* Thought*less* was the first adjective that came to mind when Sarah thought about Keith.

Lynda's phone alerted her to a text. "Steve found him," said Lynda nervously.

"Text him back; ask him to bring Keith here," directed Sarah thinking it might be better if they could talk without anyone around.

Chapter 27

Michael and Isabel concluded their meeting not long after Sarah left. Michael had Isabel's ledger with him as he exited the Main House. He wanted to drop it off at the cottage but he expected he'd find Lynda there as well; best to avoid that if he could.

He decided to walk up to the stables. It was one of two places where John Fairchild's ghost had been reported to be seen by visitors to the estate. He was also looking forward to seeing the horses, maybe they would join him in conversation again, he smiled at the thought.

He had almost made it up the hill when he saw someone he thought he knew: a few steps closer confirmed that it was Steve, his baseball conversation buddy. Steve appeared to be quite purposeful and swift in his movements, darting in and out of the stalls. Michael had a hunch that somehow Keith figured into what looked to be a search. He called out a greeting and Steve looked up.

"What brings you up here? I'm guessing you didn't come for the view," said Michael.

"No, I was hoping to find Keith up here. He seems to be AWOL," said Steve shaking his head.

"Where have you looked? I'll help," offered Michael.

"I started with the valet to be sure he hadn't left altogether. The valet couldn't answer me directly, but he did say that they hadn't brought any cars around this morning."

"That was nice of him," said Michael.

"After that I came up here and I'm thinking about going to the lake next."

"I'll tag along," said Michael, thinking fleetingly about Josiah and his crickets.

Unfortunately, the lake revealed no one sitting on its quaint little benches. The boat was still tied up at the dock and no one could be seen fishing or on the walking path that wended its way around the waterhole. After the brisk walk, both men were feeling the heat of the day.

"What now?" asked Michael.

"Damned if I know, but I promised Lynda to find him so I'm going to keep trying."

"I think we both could use a cold drink," suggested Michael.

"I know where we can get one," said Steve. "Lynda said they serve drinks in the lounge. I wouldn't presume since I'm not a registered guest, but ..."

"I am," said Michael completing the thought. "Sounds like a plan, maybe once we've cooled down, we'll figure something out."

As they walked toward the main house Steve asked Michael about the book he was carrying. Michael explained that he had indicated an interest in the history of the area and Isabel thought he might like to see it. He was relieved when Steve appeared to have no further questions on the topic.

They found Keith in the lounge, nursing a beer, and looking disgruntled. Steve and Michael sat at his table, soft drinks in hand.

"We've been looking everywhere for you, buddy," said Steve quietly. Michael said nothing, he wasn't sure he should even be there.

"Well, I've been around," said Keith sullenly. "Why are you looking for me anyway?"

"Sarah asked me to and Lynda was really upset," replied Steve.

"Who the hell is Sarah?" asked Keith, his annoyance evident.

"She's my wife," answered Michael in a tone that left nothing to the imagination.

Keith did not reply. They passed a few minutes in an uncomfortable silence. Steve ignored them both and pulled out his phone to text Lynda. He punched in his message quickly and addressed Keith.

"What's wrong with you? Are you trying to hurt Lynda?" asked Steve.

"Of course not," Keith snapped.

"Lynda said her dad lit into you over the additional charges," said Steve hoping he might start talking.

"He can afford it," said Keith, sounding like a spoiled child.

Steve sighed at this. His phone chirped and he checked his messages.

"It's from Lynda. She wants to see you. She's with Sarah in one of the cottages. From what I can see Sarah is a good friend," said Steve.

"Well, maybe I don't want to see her," said Keith petulantly.

"That's mature," said Michael. Keith shot him a look, which Michael met. Keith was the first to look away.

"When I talk to Lynda about you, she seems baffled by your behavior," said Steve, still trying to reach him. "She tells me that you've planned everything together from the beginning. You teased her about her wedding notebook, but you were there every step of the way from choosing a venue to cake tasting sessions and even flowers, man. I'm pretty sure even I'd draw the line at flowers, but she said you were sweet. What happened?"

"I don't know," said Keith looking lost. "I've felt different ever since I got here; almost like I shouldn't even be here. I'm restless, sometimes angry for no reason, and out-of-sorts. I really didn't think the band would be such a big deal and I had to invite the extra guests at the last minute, but, oh you don't care and I don't blame you. I've been doing other stupid and impulsive things, too. It's why I cancelled breakfast; I was going to try to fix another blunder."

Neither Steve or Michael cared to follow-up on that comment. This was the first time Michael felt anything other than distaste for the groom. He knew first-hand about hosting unwanted feelings and wondered if he and Keith had more in common than he expected.

Steve was still intent on his mission.

"Are you ready to talk with Lynda?" he asked pocketing his phone.

"What can I say to her?" asked a more subdued Keith.

"If it was Sarah I'd best start with an apology," said Michael.

Chapter 28

Steve took his leave after he was sure that Keith and Lynda were reunited. Sarah and Michael left them to talk in their cottage in private. However, they both agreed that they would like to be a fly on the wall to hear that discussion.

While they waited, they took a stroll off the gravel path into the trees where it would be cooler. Sarah noticed that Michael seemed distracted and gave him a few minutes before asking, "Did you learn anything new from Isabel?"

"Well, she did give me her ledger and said it also includes sightings from members of the overnight staff here on the plantation. I thought you might like to take a look at it."

"Don't you want to look through it, too?" she asked.

"Sure, but you're the librarian," he answered with a smile.

"I'll take a look when we get back into the cottage," said Sarah. "I found out that Lynda's father is *the* Fuller of Fuller Real Estate Solutions."

Michael recognized the name at once. "Wow. Impressive."

"Yeah, and to think I was worried about Lynda getting in too deep financially with wedding costs."

"Silly you," said Michael with his trademark twinkle.

"I wonder what's going to happen," said Sarah thoughtfully.

S. L. SUMNER

"No idea," Michael shrugged. He was still wondering about Keith's comments to Steve about feeling angry and out-of-sorts. "It was odd ..." Michael began but hesitated.

"What was odd?" asked Sarah.

"Keith said he felt different ever since he arrived here; he said he felt like he shouldn't *be* here. That's an odd thing to say."

"Yes, it is," Sarah allowed.

"He also said he's been feeling angry and out-of-sorts for no reason."

"Are you thinking he's having second thoughts?"

"No, I was thinking something else."

Sarah looked at him. It took a moment but eventually the coin dropped. She flashed back to angry Michael obsessed with seeing those pearl-handled pistols.

"Have we misjudged Keith?" she asked.

Michael shrugged. He wasn't sure what to think.

Chapter 29

After her meeting with Michael, Isabel went to her desk to check her emails. She made short work of them and then went downstairs to meet with Keith's musicians. She was concerned that they might prove difficult if Keith himself was any indication. She didn't mind live musicians but she hadn't heard of this group and thought it would have been easier to work with someone familiar. Even the DJ, who wasn't her favorite, was at least known to her and she knew he would come with everything he needed.

She was pleasantly surprised when she found them to be charming, organized and fully prepared. She showed them where they would set up, asked them if there was anything she needed to supply, and arranged a time for them to arrive.

Next, she went to the Main Hall to see the florists who were placing flowers on the canopy where the vows would be exchanged. It was coming along nicely. They informed her that delivery of arrangements for the tables in the Ballroom was scheduled for the following morning. A brief conversation about where to deliver the bouquets and boutonnieres and arrangements for their final payment concluded their business. Another item on her check-list completed.

Work was going smoothly, but she was often distracted by thoughts of Michael's many experiences here at the estate. It occurred to her that she would miss hearing about his encounters when he checked out on Sunday. She wondered if he would keep in touch, or, if he might someday return to visit the estate. She was fascinated by his abilities and it didn't hurt that he seemed to be both charming and kind.

Jonah appeared in her office at 3:30. She was pleased when he showed up earlier than she had requested. They talked about his experience the previous night and he repeated that he understood about keeping the incident confidential. She thanked him for agreeing to work both Friday and Saturday evenings.

The only remaining difficulty was staffing the sit-down dinner for the reception. She still needed to replace one of the servers, maybe two, if Cindy decided to turn in her resignation. She picked up the phone to go through her list of possible fill-in wait staff one more time. It was not one of her favorite tasks so she took a few minutes to prepare a cup of tea.

She phoned the last name on her list before she was able to fill the opening. She then decided to phone Cindy to see whether they would be short a waitress or not. A few moments later she happily crossed another item off her to-do list. Cindy had already decided that she had been overreacting. She even blamed Jonah for "setting the mood" with his insistence on the need for both of them to deliver the pillows. Isabel decided not to call her on this, at least not until after the wedding reception. Full staffing for a sit-down dinner would make the evening go much more smoothly. For the moment, this outweighed the need for a conversation about Cindy's apparent ability to set aside the rules.

Isabel checked her watch, she still had time to check in with the valets before the off-site guests began to arrive. She rounded the corner of the main house on her way to the carriage house when she saw him. It had been a while, but she recognized him immediately. She wondered if he would talk to her, she'd never tried before.

"Good afternoon," she said as she drew near. She could feel her heart rate pulsing more rapidly while she waited for his reply. "It's a little warm to be pulling weeds."

Josiah looked up from his work. "Yes ma'am," he said.

Oh my God, he answered me! What do I say now?

"You have a talent for working with the gardens."

"Thank you, ma'am."

*I am **talking** with Josiah!*

"I understand you've met one of our guests."

"Ma'am?" *Was she imagining that Josiah looked worried?*

"Oh, it's alright," she assured him, "he's enjoyed your conversations."

Her reassurance appeared to have little effect. She decided it would be best to conclude the interaction.

"Well, keep up the good work. I'm off to the carriage house to chat with – uh Miss Phoebe." She was going to say "the valets about tonight's parking" but thought better of it. She resumed her stroll toward the carriage house.

"Ma'am?" Josiah called after her.

"Yes?" Her heart picked up the beat once again.

"Folks on my side is all stirred up, jus' all stirred up," he told her shaking his head. She could see something like resignation in his eyes, but mostly fear.

"I know, Josiah."

"Mebbe you kin warn tha young fella...?"

"I will," said Isabel, "I'll tell him." She continued in the direction of the carriage house, certain that if she looked back, he would be gone.

Chapter 30

It had been an eventful day. Sarah said she wasn't surprised when Lynda and Keith told them that the rehearsal would go on as planned. Michael, however, thought he detected a little dismay at the news.

Sarah pinned her brooch to the bottom of her high collar and admired herself in the mirror. She remarked that she thought it complemented her outfit beautifully and looked forward to sharing its connection to the estate with her friends from the library.

Michael didn't seem to be listening so she tried again, "Well, what do you think, dear?" she asked Michael modeling her ensemble.

"Oh! It looks great. What a thoughtful and charming husband you have!"

"I guess I have to agree," said Sarah adding, "and so modest, too."

"You look beautiful, Sarah," said Michael sincerely. He offered his arm and asked, "Shall we go?"

THE REHEARSAL TOOK place in the ballroom. They started late, at about a quarter past five as they waited for the tardy groom to arrive. Hoping that wasn't a bad sign Sarah and Michael sat in the second row waiting for the proceedings to begin. Sarah also still wanted to keep an eye on Joanna, who, at least, had been on time.

There were only a handful of guests for the rehearsal although Lynda's father had generously opened the dinner to all the guests who had traveled for the wedding. As soon as everyone was in their places. Steve walked down the aisle and seated Lynda's mother in the front row. He then went up and stood next to Keith. They did not include music for the rehearsal so Joanna, as maid of honor, walked in silence toward the officiant where Lynda and Keith would exchange faux vows. Sarah hoped she imagined the look exchanged between Joanna and the groom who stood waiting for his bride. After Joanna took her place to the left of the bridal canopy Isabel cued the bride and her father to begin their walk down the aisle. Sarah noted that the expression on Lynda's face was not the light-hearted look of happy anticipation that most brides-to-be wore for their rehearsal; her smile was not so much radiant as nervous. The expression on her father's face could only be described as neutral, perhaps it was the best he could manage given all of Keith's surprises. When they reached the front of the room her father stiffly kissed her cheek and took a seat next to her mother.

The ceremony would be led by Reverend Martha Vaughan, a Stokes family friend. She smiled and she said she would have a few opening remarks before the vows were exchanged, but they would have to wait until the ceremony to hear her nuggets of wisdom. A few chuckled at her facetious tone. Sarah saw an unmistakable eye roll from Joanna at this announcement.

Michael was waiting to see if the phrase, "speak now or forever hold your peace" would be included. He'd been to many weddings where it was not used. Apparently, Rev. Vaughan was a traditionalist. Michael glanced at Sarah who was watching for reactions to the phrase. Keith feigned a worried look which got a laugh from Joanna and a couple of others in attendance. Even the minister smiled, rehearsals were often full of silly levity, a sort of release before the solemn occasion to follow.

They then practiced their vows; Keith's remarks were brief and his attempts to be humorous fell far short of the mark. Only Joanna seemed to find them amusing. Lynda stared at her feet and blushed at his lack of decorum. By contrast, Lynda's voice was soft and nervous during her portion. At one point Keith told her to "Pick up the pace, dear, I'm hungry" which evoked a snort and laughter from Joanna and one or two others. Before the rings were exchanged Steve whispered something to Keith which could not be heard to which he muttered loud enough for all to hear, "Where's your sense of humor?"

It was during the exchange of rings that Michael saw someone whose name was definitely *not* on the guest list. Standing just behind Keith was the bloody soldier still in agony, blood still slowly pulsing from his abdomen, his face contorted in a soundless scream. Michael looked at Sarah in alarm. She returned his look questioningly before she began the now familiar fading from his sight.

Now in a mostly empty ballroom rain poured down from the ceiling. Michael took a breath and steeled himself for the expected wave of emotion. He watched the soldier carefully. Before Keith disappeared, it looked as though he had been the target of the ghost's shock and dismay. Now without Keith the scene took on a different aspect for across the room stood a man holding an ivory handled pistol which was smoking as though recently fired. This specter was an abomination. He wore a suit covered by a cloak to protect him from the downpour. His clothing was disintegrating, his skin wrinkled and dry much like shriveled leather. His face was distorted with dark brown eyes that exuded rage and utter disappointment. Michael recoiled from the onslaught of anger and bitter sadness that he now shared with the specter. Those eyes, which had been locked on the soldier, unlocked themselves and slowly turned in Michael's direction as he knew they would. Michael prayed he was prepared to meet them. He steeled himself to withstand both the soldier's shock and fear and John Fairchild's outrage and disappointment simultaneously. He thought about the contents of the note trying to remember it word for word, he pictured the locket in his mind as he pushed against the wave of rage which tried to overtake him and concentrated on what *he* needed to convey.

"I do not wish to come between a loving father and his beloved daughter. I now wish I had chosen to fight for the South against my own father's wishes, for I would rather have lost the war than my chance to share your love."

After what seemed an eternity, the man dropped the gun, fell to his knees, and covered his face with his withered hands in apparent despair.

"Michael," whispered Sarah urgently, "Are you alright?"

Michael pushed through the layers that separated him from the ghosts of the past and fought his way back to Sarah. The now familiar pulling sensation was welcome because it meant the end of the episode. He soon found himself seated on the wooden folding chair that had been behind him as he stood to watch the rehearsal. He had no recollection of sitting, but he was grateful not to be collapsed in a heap on the floor. Several of the guests were standing over him, one of them a doctor offering his services. Michael was dismayed to note that the proceedings seemed to have been halted.

"I'm fine," he managed to say, adding, "so sorry to cause such a disruption."

"Oh, never mind that," said Lynda kindly, "We just want to be sure you're okay."

"I am," he assured her, "but I'm sorry to have caused any sort of distress to such a beautiful bride on the eve of her special day." Even in his embarrassment, he hoped Keith might take note of the proper way to treat a lady.

Lynda's smile was in earnest. "Oh, I bet you say that to all the brides," she replied.

Sarah made up a story about low blood sugar and she and Michael were excused to get a little something in his stomach. They made their way out of the ballroom guided by Isabel who had also been keeping an eye on things. Instead of going into the main dining hall Isabel guided them into a small office nearby.

"Geez, what happened?" asked Michael, "Did I make a total fool of myself?"

"Not really," replied Sarah "you looked like you'd taken ill, gasped, and then sat down really abruptly. I did my part just making sure you sat on the chair instead of the floor. It wasn't easy!"

"Well, I think I can now add John Fairchild to my collection of ghosts," said Michael after they settled into chairs. "I think I saw something similar to my dream yesterday afternoon."

"In the dream with the lady and her tea? You didn't mention it before," noted Sarah.

"I didn't remember it then. I remember it pretty damn clearly now though. In the dream he just looked like the silhouette of a man. What I saw in the ballroom was a different story, same intense dark brown eyes though. Another thing, Lydia was in my dream but she was in the stables. I'm wondering if she witnessed the shooting. Do you know if she did, Isabel?"

"No, I'm afraid I don't," replied Isabel. "Michael, I'm so sorry; I tried to catch up with you before the rehearsal; I wanted to talk with you about something that happened this afternoon."

"It's okay," said Michael. He could see she was upset. "What happened?

"I saw Josiah. We spoke," she waited for his reaction. He smiled, encouraging her to continue with his eyes.

"And?"

"He wanted me to warn you; he said that "folks on his side are all worked up".

"Tell me something I *don't* know."

"Can you describe the vision?" asked Isabel.

"I saw the soldier first; he looked just as he did when I saw him in the library. He had been shot. I also saw John, at least I think it must have been John, holding the gun which must have just been fired because it was smoking and I could smell the sulfur odor of the gunpowder. It seemed like they were frozen in that moment just after John pulled the trigger but before the soldier falls after being hit. The biggest impression is a mix of very intense, almost overwhelming, emotions. The surprise, disbelief and fear of the soldier coupled with John's sense of having been betrayed, his rage at all Yankees being directed at this one young man, and his ultimate despair over his daughter's pain all combined into a crushing wave of intense feelings. Last time it happened I thought about the locket the dog found and it seemed to ease the emotions I was feeling from the soldier. This time I did my best to recall the contents of the note we found and how James didn't want to come between Lydia and her father. I was hoping that it might help John in some way to know about it. At any rate the vision did finally come to an end. How long was it?"

"Not long," answered Sarah, "at first you looked scared to death, then you just sort of 'checked out'. I don't think anyone noticed anything was going on until your legs just folded up and you sat down hard on the chair. Even then you just sat there with that glazed look on your face for a few moments longer; I whispered your name several times before you responded."

"Did they ever finish the rehearsal?"

"Not before we left the room," said Sarah.

"I guess I should probably get back to them," said Isabel. "I may have some smoothing over to do. Stay here as long as you wish."

"Before you go, we've been meaning to ask you, which of the bedrooms belonged to Lydia?" said Sarah.

"Her room was just above the sitting room at the front of the house," answered Isabel.

"Do you know which guest is using it this weekend?" Sarah asked.

"We use it for brides because the lighting is perfect for photographs in the afternoons. Lynda is using it this weekend," replied Isabel.

In the end they didn't stay long, deciding to attend the rehearsal dinner. For one thing, they were hungry, and, for another, Sarah was still interested in observing Joanna. She was beginning to suspect who she had been with in the stables, but not sure what to do if she was able to confirm it. Michael was just happy she didn't seem too rattled by Josiah's warning.

They found their seats at one of the large round tables. Several people came over to say they hoped Michael was feeling better.

Lynda and Keith stopped to say hello. Lynda was solicitous as always. Keith simply said, "Told ya to lay off the sauce big fella," which did not do much to repair Sarah's opinion of him. Michael glared at him for a moment before remembering that he needed to be considerate of the bride.

Steve stopped by their table as well. He said he hoped Michael's evening would improve and that the meal would be served soon.

"So how are you doing with your duties as Best Man?" asked Michael.

"I'm just glad it will be over soon," said Steve looking like he wished he were anywhere else.

"That bad?" asked Michael.

Steve took the seat next to Michael and said softly, "I just never really knew what a jerk Keith can be. We went to college together and played sports and stuff. You expect that sort of locker room mentality when guys get together, but it seems like he's never outgrown it. He's been making a real mess of things this weekend, but he doesn't seem to realize it or care. I don't like the way he's been treating Lynda. I mean, I only just met her, but she seems nice and he just keeps making everything difficult for her."

"Can you talk to him?"

"I've tried to a little, but we haven't seen each other in years. Frankly I was surprised when he asked me to be his best man. My parents live just outside Atlanta so I thought why not? I thought I could combine the trip with a little family time. Both Keith and Lynda said they were keeping the guest list small so it seemed like it might be a simple affair. This is anything but simple," he ended ruefully.

"Quit," said Michael simply.

"What?"

"Just quit," repeated Michael, "Leave him in the lurch. Let him see what it feels like to be on the receiving end of thoughtless behavior." It was what Michael would do in his shoes.

"He wouldn't get the message," protested Steve, "and where would that leave Lynda?"

"She has more to worry about with the groom than with the best man."

"I really thought I was getting through to him this afternoon. I guess not. I'd hate to create even more trouble for Lynda," Steve winced at the thought.

"Oh, 'cause it's going to be such fun to be married to a rude, thoughtless, self-centered jerk," said Michael with a wry smile. "Maybe this is what she needs to see him more clearly."

"When you put it that way," Steve smiled for the first time. He seemed to be considering Michael's suggestion. "You may have a point," he said before standing and walking away in the direction of the groom-to-be.

Chapter 31

It was a most uncomfortable evening. Lynda was not able to mask her disappointment standing in front of her closest friends and family as Keith continued to make light of what she considered a serious commitment. This broke her father's heart and made it impossible for him to maintain his neutral façade. He sat scowling at his seat to the left of the maid of honor. Her mother was shy in the best of circumstances. Michael thought she looked like a turtle desperately searching for a shell to crawl into.

Rehearsal dinners are mostly about toasts and tearful tributes. Michael thought about the "toast" offered by Keith at the Welcome Dinner and hoped tonight's tributes would not follow in a similar vein. He considered the head table: Keith's parents who acted as if all was well, the "happy" couple, one bored maid of honor, and the downcast parents of the bride-to-be. The chair for the best man was empty. Waiters were circulating with champagne to prepare for the first toasts of the evening.

Since the best man had not appeared Keith's father stood to make the first toast. He shared a few cherished childhood memories, complimented the bride, and talked about his son's finer attributes. After that he just kept talking almost as though stalling for time. Sarah began to fidget in her seat, she was not one to listen to rambling speeches. Michael patted her hand realizing her growing impatience.

She finally whispered very softly, "Finish already!"

Michael whispered back, "Steve isn't here."

Sarah sat up straighter and slowly took in the room. "Where did he go?" Michael did not reply but the guilty look on his face told Sarah that something was up. "What did you do?"

"We'll talk later," said Michael, as enigmatic as the Sphinx.

At last Keith's dad ran out of accolades and everyone raised a glass to the groom. Lynda's father stood next. He spoke glowingly of his lovely daughter, but said not one word about his soon-to-be son-in-law. He finished quickly and all in the room toasted the tearful bride. Tears, happy or heart-broken, are not uncommon at wedding toasts, but by now it was clear that the best man was not coming. Keith looked slightly lost and Michael noted that his ears, of all things, appeared bright red. There was a quick whispered exchange between Lynda, her maid of honor, and the groom before Lynda stood and announced that the meal would soon be served and she hoped everyone would eat, drink and be merry.

The rehearsal dinner buffet was aiming for a bit of fun. Guests could choose from three entrees: Fried Chicken and Waffles, Barbecue Pulled Pork, or a Grilled Vegetable Platter for those in need of a meatless option. Both Michael and Sarah chose the pulled pork which came with a small brown ramekin of baked beans, corn on the cob and Texas toast. Salads, desserts, and beverages would be served by the wait staff.

Sarah and Michael made their way to their seats at a table for ten among friends and co-workers from the library. Salads had been served and table conversation was superficial: the weather is hot, the venue is beautiful, etc. Side conversations were quiet but rather more animated as guests wondered and offered ideas about the missing bridal party member, shared observations about Keith's behavior, and worried aloud about their friend.

Sarah watched Michael finish a bite of pork before asking, "Is it later?"

Michael looked around the room. When he was satisfied that no one was listening he turned to Sarah.

"Steve told me he was unhappy with how Keith was treating Lynda and that he wasn't enjoying the role of being his best man. I told him to quit, you know, show him how it feels when people let you down. I didn't think he really would though." Michael watched his wife's reaction carefully for signs of annoyance. They paused their conversation while the waiter offered coffee.

"I thought you'd never ask," Sarah told the waiter with a grateful smile before turning to Michael to add, "Hmmm, interesting. What else did he say about Lynda?" she asked.

Relieved, he replied, "He said he couldn't bear to cause her hurt. He was worried that his sudden absence would just add to all the trouble Keith has caused."

"See, I think he kind of likes Lynda!" said Sarah excited that her theory might prove to be accurate. Michael was just happy she didn't consider it meddling.

"So, you're not upset with me?" He needed confirmation and risked asking the question he might not want to hear the answer to.

"Nope, serves him right. The more I see of Keith the less I like him. I'm convinced that this marriage won't last. Lynda is just snake-bit when it comes to relationships. When I think about all the break-ups – you know I have to work with her and she just gets so down on herself. I think she tries too hard to please. Something you could never say about me!" she ended with a laugh at her own expense.

"You're not so bad, dear, as long as I do as I'm told."

"I think I need to visit with the bride, why don't you see if you can locate our missing best man?" directed Sarah taking a gulp of coffee before standing and dropping her napkin on her plate.

HAVING BEEN GIVEN HIS marching orders Michael went in search of Steve. Problem was, he had no idea where to look, he wasn't even sure if Steve was still on the estate since he had family living nearby. He left the dining room and saw Isabel in the hallway directing some waiters to begin serving dessert. He looked at the dessert trays; it appeared to be a choice between peach cobbler and some variation of pecan pie. They looked perfectly delicious, just like all the other menus and amenities that had been provided to guests. Michael thought it a shame that the groom was spoiling an otherwise splendid event. Once the waiters were dispatched to the dining room Isabel turned her attention to Michael.

"Good evening," she said with a tinge of doubt in her tone, "Is everything alright? You haven't ..."

"No, I'm fine," replied Michael cutting off her question. "I was wondering if you have seen Steve, the best man."

"No, but I am aware that he is not in attendance. I did see him leave after a brief conversation with the groom. At the time I just thought he was on some kind of errand and would return. Looks like I was wrong about that."

"Which way did he go? I hope to catch up to him."

"I think he left the main house; you might ask the valets if they brought a car around for anyone."

Michael considered how much of his day had been spent trying to find AWOL bridal party members as he headed out into the coolness of the summer evening. Being from central Florida he marveled at how cool the evenings were even in July once the sun dipped below the hills. He strode past the gardens and thought of Josiah. Turning the corner he saw a silhouette of someone just off the path. His first thought was of the shadowy likeness of John Fairchild from his dream but as he got nearer, he thought he recognized the body posture: It was Steve.

"Ah, here you are!" he said hoping to convey a friend-not-foe tone in the darkness. "I was hoping to find you, I thought maybe you left."

"I almost did," replied Steve, "but I wanted to know what happened, and, uh, I wanted to know if Lynda is ..." He had run out of words.

"She seems to be handling it. It was Lynda who made an announcement to guests after both fathers made remarks. May I ask what you said to Keith?"

"I told him I wouldn't be staying for dinner and suggested he might want to start treating Lynda in a manner she deserves if he wanted a best man at his wedding. As I expected, he seemed a little surprised and slightly confused, but on the whole unconcerned about my exit."

They had been walking in the general direction of the carriage house so Michael asked if he might like to stop in at their cottage for a drink. Steve gratefully accepted saying he could use one. Michael texted Sarah to let her know where she could find them.

Chapter 32

S arah wended her way through the tables making a path to the head table. Guests had begun to mingle a bit, visiting other tables here and there as desserts and coffee were served. Only Lynda and her parents remained at the main table. Keith's parents could be seen at a nearby table chatting. She couldn't locate Keith anywhere and didn't really care, in fact, she was grateful for his absence because she couldn't trust herself not to give him a piece of her mind. She spent a few moments making small talk with Lynda's parents and then took Joanna's seat next to Lynda who sat quietly moving a slice of pecan pie around with her fork.

"Dinner was a real treat. This place does such a nice job; everything has been really top-notch," Sarah offered.

"Has it? I'm glad," replied Lynda, but she didn't sound glad. Then she seemed to remember about Michael and asked after him.

"He's fine," replied Sarah. "I've sent him on a mission. He's probably sorry to be missing these lovely desserts."

"A mission?"

"Oh, never mind him, how are *you*? Would you like to have a good chat after the meal? I could come up to your room and we could raid the mini bar."

"Yes, I need to sort some things out and it might be helpful to hear what you think."

Sarah thought she might do better to keep her opinion to herself until she heard Lynda's thoughts. She could thread the needle between total candor and enabling support for what she now worried would be a big mistake. If Lynda was beginning to question this match Sarah hoped she would say so and allow her to support her. A waiter arrived with coffee and Sarah considered the cobbler that had been left untouched at Joanna's place. She picked up a fresh fork, looked over at her friend who nodded approval, shrugged, and took a bite.

SARAH AND LYNDA SAT on the bed in Lynda's room with two ice-filled glasses. Sarah found a can of ginger ale and a tiny bottle of Dewar's in the minifridge. She divided the Scotch between both glasses and poured the ginger ale over the ice. Soon they each sipped on a highball.

"Ah, that is good!" declared Sarah.

"Yes, this was a good idea," agreed Lynda.

Lynda took a sip, kicked the shoes off her feet and leaned back on the pillows.

"Your brooch is very pretty," she remarked. "I've been admiring it since you sat with me after dinner."

"Thank you. Michael bought it for me at a little antique shop nearby. The woman there told him that it belonged to Lydia Fairchild of Southern Oak and the Fairchild Estate. It even has the initials L.F. on the back." She unpinned it from her dress to show it to her friend.

"My initials are L.F.," Lynda said thoughtfully, "at least until tomorrow after the wedding, if there is a wedding."

"Are you really thinking of calling it off?" asked Sarah.

"Oh, I don't know," Lynda said sadly, "maybe Keith wants to call it off. He isn't acting like he much cares about my feelings."

"Michael told me that Keith admitted that he's been feeling angry and out-of-sorts since he arrived here," Sarah said.

"Well, it would be nice if he shared that with me; did he also say he was feeling like an ass?"

"What did you talk about with him this afternoon?" Sarah was surprised that he hadn't told her how he's been feeling.

"He apologized, several times, but he didn't really explain anything. I hoped he would. I'm not used to this new version of Keith, but he promised to do better and I told him it was okay. Now, I'm not sure why I said that. What else could I say? It's a little late to be calling things off."

Sarah compared this passive version of Lynda to the version she knew from work. Lynda, Director of Programming, was anything but passive. That Lynda was a non-nonsense organizer who knew how to network, solve problems and get her plans into place. This version was vulnerable and meek. She was finding it hard to reconcile the two. She thought about the large notebook Sarah used for years to plan her wedding. It had sections for caterers, florists, musicians, venues, dresses, and even one for honeymoon destinations. So much thought and planning and now everything was coming apart.

"Well, I only know this version of Keith who appears to be very different from the fellow you've been happily dating. It's hard for me to say, but I will say that the Keith I have met is not someone I can see you being happy with. The question is, which Keith are you marrying?"

They were quiet for a few minutes and Sarah took the opportunity to look around the room. She was interested in the hardwood floors and noted a braided rug in the center of the room.

"Did you know this house has a very interesting history?" Sarah asked deciding a change of topic was in order. "Michael has been talking to Isabel about the estate and the family who lived here during the Civil War."

"Yes, I've even heard the rumors about ghosts."

"You have?!" Sarah was surprised.

"Oh yeah, Isabel and I met at a symposium a few years ago and we talked about our jobs. She made mine seem rather boring."

"I didn't know you knew her before now."

"Sure, I direct programming at the library and she's an event planner. We met at the Planning Symposium in Orlando a few years back and we've kept in touch. She told me a few juicy stories about this place. I'm not sure I believe in it, but she definitely seems open to it."

"Well, I think Michael has become more open to the idea since coming here," said Sarah.

"Really?" Lynda sat up with interest. "What makes you say that?"

Sarah paused before answering, "Well, he didn't have a blood sugar episode tonight."

"Really?! Was it a …?"

"Vision of some sort, yeah," Sarah completed the thought.

"Wow, I wondered when you said blood sugar, you've never mentioned anything about him being diabetic. That's amazing, tell me what happened." For the first time since the weekend began Lynda was not worrying about wedding details.

"He said he saw a soldier who had been shot and the man who shot him. And yesterday he took a nap and had a strange dream about a woman stirring a cup of tea; she was worried that someone named Lydia was unhappy. Lydia was the name of the Fairchild's youngest child and, I think, the original owner of my brooch. Michael's been sharing his experiences with Isabel and they were wondering if Lydia may have hidden a diary or something in her room somewhere."

"Isabel told me about the scandal of the Fairchild Family, but she said most of the allegations could not be proven. The story is that his daughter fell in love with a Yankee soldier and her father did not approve. When a Yankee soldier was killed trespassing on his land everyone just filled in the blanks. There's no proof for any of it. I can't figure out how he managed to explain away the murder and get off Scott-free. He should have had to stand trial if you ask me," said Lynda.

"I guess things were different back then," said Sarah who wished Lynda could take a similar hard line when it came to Keith.

"So he thinks there could be some kind of proof hidden in her room?" asked Lynda.

"Not proof exactly, but maybe a diary or something. I kept a diary as a girl, did you?"

"Of course," said Lynda, "I still have all of mine. Which room was Lydia's?"

"This is Lydia's room," said Sarah. Lynda's eyes widened. She looked at her surroundings as if seeing them for the first time.

Sarah stood and walked to the edge of the braided rug and lifted it. They both tapped at the floor beneath it hoping to discover a loose board, but it seemed quite solid.

Sarah had her phone on silent but she recognized its muffled buzz and went to retrieve it from her handbag. She had a text from Michael.

Where RU?

With Lynda in her room.

Find anything?

Just started looking. Where R U?

Our cottage with Steve

Good!

"Is he alright?" asked Lynda.

"Yes, and he completed his mission," replied Sarah smiling.

"Which was ...?"

"He's back at our cottage with Steve."

"He is?!"

"I asked him to see if he could find him. I don't think it was easy for Steve to walk out like he did."

"No, I don't suppose it was," agreed Lynda.

Sarah's phone summoned her again.

Would u like to join us?

"He wants to know if we'd like to join them."

Lynda considered the offer a moment before answering.

"Tell them we'll join them soon. I want to poke around the room to see if we can find anything first."

We'll be there in about half an hour, will Steve wait for us?

He says he will

Okay, see you then.

OK <3 U

Sarah and Lynda surveyed the room. Sarah looked under the big four poster bed while Lynda tapped the walls searching for a hollow sound that might indicate a hidden niche. Both came up empty.

"Well, none of the floor boards seem loose to me," said Sarah, discouraged.

"I wonder if any of this furniture was here when it was Lydia's room. They look like antiques, but they might be replicas since this place gets a lot of use from guests."

"That desk looks pretty old," said Sarah.

Unfortunately, the desk was empty except for some Southern Oak stationery, a pen, and a brochure about the estate. A thorough search didn't reveal any false bottomed drawers or hidden compartments.

"So much for that," said Lynda laughing. "I'd have been surprised to find anything."

Sarah wasn't quite ready to give up. "What about that dresser?" she asked.

"It's called a chiffonier," said Lynda "at least that's what Isabel said. I haven't used it because I found a silverfish in one of the drawers. I just hung most of my things and have kept everything else in my suitcases."

In spite of the silverfish Sarah thought the piece was exquisite. Seven drawers tall, it had a pull-out top on the third drawer from the bottom that could be used as a writing surface. Four more drawers sat atop the first three. Sarah used the two drawer pulls to tug the piece out. The top had a blue velour inset that could be used as a writing surface. Sarah pulled it out a little further but stopped at the sound of paper crinkling like the crunch of crisp potato chips. She looked at Lynda who was wincing at the sound.

"Sounds like paper tearing," said Sarah

"I wonder ..." Sarah pulled until the piece would not slide any further. "I hoped it would come all the way out. Then maybe we could see what made the sound."

"Pull out the drawer below it," suggested Lynda.

Sarah pushed the top piece back in and pulled out the drawer below it.

Now that the top was removed from the drawer, they could see an envelope pressed against the back and side. Sarah lifted it out and tried to smooth it back into something resembling its original shape. There was no writing on the outside of the envelope; it was torn and she could see a sheet of paper inside.

"I think it's time to join the gentlemen in the Magnolia Cottage," said Sarah, "I know Michael will want to see this."

Chapter 33

Since Steve had missed dinner Michael ordered a couple of Reuben sandwiches and chips from the room service menu. Michael considered telling him about some of his experiences, but resisted the impulse thinking that Steve had enough on his plate without adding a supernatural twist.

They chatted for a while about Keith's odd behavior and Lynda's apparent willingness to overlook his impulsive behavior. Steve was trying to make up his mind about whether to continue his boycott or participate in the ceremony in spite of everything.

"How can he seem so vulnerable and contrite one minute and then act so rude and flippant the next?" asked Steve.

"And why is Lynda putting up with it?" asked Michael.

"Maybe she's the reticent type," suggested Steve.

"Not according to Sarah. She says she's organized, efficient and a no-nonsense type at work." Michael had his own theory but he wasn't ready to share it since there was little to support it; he was also a bit resistant to giving up his image of Keith as a selfish jerk. He decided to compromise on his position.

"I know I'm the one who told you to quit, but you're also the only guest, aside from Sarah, to provide me with any interesting conversation so far. I want you to hang around for purely selfish reasons." He was careful to use the word, "guest" since he'd had enlightening chats with Isabel and unusually engaging exchanges with Josiah.

By the time Sarah and Lynda arrived they were back to talking baseball, this time a rousing conversation about the success of franchises with deep pockets versus those with more limited resources. Michael was enjoying himself enough that when Sarah delayed their arrival for an additional 30 minutes he was secretly pleased for the extra time.

Sarah was eager to share the contents of the letter which she had resisted opening until they were together. She waited, however, until greetings were exchanged watching carefully when Steve asked Lynda how she was doing. Each time she saw them together she was more convinced that there was chemistry.

Eventually Michael asked about the envelope Sarah was carrying.

"I've been waiting for you to ask," she told him before adding, "I haven't looked at it yet, we found it in a dresser in Lynda's room."

Michael took the envelope and opened it carefully. He could see that it was fragile. It appeared to be a note, but unfinished. He read it aloud:

FATHER,

Please forgive me for not saying my farewell in person. I know you disagree with my choice, but I cannot bear to be parted from James. If the war had not interfered with our lives, you would have blessed our union. I hope you know how much I love you, but as it stands now

"As it stands now – what?" asked Sarah.

"That's it, that's all there is," said Michael.

"I wonder if Isabel can tell us if it's Lydia's handwriting," said Lynda.

"What are you all talking about?" asked Steve looking confused.

Michael looked at Sarah, not knowing how to answer.

"Well, the short version is that there is a scandal associated with the owners of Southern Oak. The daughter of a Colonel in the Confederacy was believed to have fallen in love with a Yankee soldier shortly after the war's end. Dad did not approve, to put it mildly. The former soldier was shot and killed, admittedly by the Colonel, ostensibly for trespassing on his land. Shortly after, his daughter also died, of unknown causes." Sarah was a master at succinct summaries.

"I see," said Steve, although he still looked a bit lost.

"There's evidence for all of it except the secret liaison between Lydia and the soldier. This note, if it's in Lydia's handwriting, would support the theory that they had been meeting secretly," she explained.

"And you found it? Tonight?" asked Steve.

"Yes, in the chiffonier in my room," said Lynda.

"The chiff-what?" asked Steve.

"Chiffonier," said Lynda laughing, "it's a dresser."

"But why were you searching her room?" asked Steve.

There was a noticeable silence as all three considered an answer to this question. Sarah was the first to speak.

"Michael has taken an interest in the history of the plantation; he's been talking with Isabel who shared some of her research with him," she explained.

"I still don't get why you were searching in Lynda's room."

"Because Lynda's room used to be Lydia's room," answered Sarah.

"Oh," said Steve seemingly satisfied with this answer.

Eventually the conversation returned to the rehearsal dinner party and Steve's absence. Steve tried to apologize, but Lynda stopped him.

"There's nothing to apologize for," she told him, "Keith made a mess of the evening, not you. I applaud you for not putting up with it. I should take a page from your book." She gave him a little hug as if to emphasize the point.

"Now, I really should be going," said Lynda, "one way or another, tomorrow will be a big day."

"Let me see you back to your room; it's late to be out walking alone," offered Steve.

Chapter 34

I sabel was reasonably pleased with the evening. She realized that there were problems brewing between the bride-to-be and her betrothed, but those things were not within her control. In spite of some boorish behavior by the groom and Mr. Daniels' episode, the evening had gone as well as it possibly could.

After the last guest left, she checked with the head waiter to be sure that he had everything he needed in terms of staff. They would need to clean up the main dining room and prep the ballroom for tomorrow's wedding reception before they left. She knew that the work was left in good hands, no need to micromanage.

She called to ask that her car be brought around to the front instead of walking back to the employee parking area. She often did this after a planned evening event because of the lateness of the hour and today had been a very busy day. If she was honest, however, she might admit that she was avoiding another possible chat with Josiah.

It felt good to be off her feet as she settled in behind the wheel. Instead of driving toward the exit she took the path to the carriage house and on toward the cottages. One last unofficial task to end her day: she wanted to drive past Magnolia to see if all was well. As she approached the cottage, she noted how dimly the lights shone. It was as if the windows were draped by black gauze. She slowed to try to see more clearly. Now she could imagine them to be shadows as Jonah had described. One hovered at every window of the cottage, its lights now barely visible. She drove past the building looking for a spot to turn around. The evening was cool so she had the windows down to feel the night air. It was late; the silence was unnatural. After executing a U-turn she strained her ears to hear anything, only the hum of the engine registered. She stopped and cut the engine, listening intently. Absolute silence. She restarted her car and continued cautiously, pressing the button to close the window as she drove.

HER HEART RATE QUICKENED and her palms were moist. As the cottage came back into view, she was surprised that the windows appeared to be free of shadows, their lights shining brightly. The path in front of her, however, suddenly seemed to be a wall of blackness. There was no other way to describe it. She strained to see the edge of the gravel path, worried if she proceeded, she might run off the edge. She would not describe what she was now seeing as shadows, it seemed almost solid. She wasn't sure how long she sat there afraid to continue, trying to make sense of what she was seeing, trying to understand the sense of gloom that was descending. At length there was a change. She watched in awe as the thing pulled itself into pieces that glided back toward the windows of Magnolia Cottage.

She stopped on the path in front of Magnolia, leaving the engine running and the headlights burning brightly. She reminded herself that no one had ever reported being harmed during their experiences on the premises and opened the car door.

The shadows seemed to register the movement immediately pulling back from the windows. Now it seemed a better plan to remain in the car; she reached for her cell instead. She was inundated by an uncanny, ominous presence. She phoned the carriage house and steadied her voice to ask them to connect her to Magnolia. Michael answered. He sounded much like she felt.

"Hello?"

"It's Isabel, I'm outside in my car."

"Are you?"

"Yes, there is no shadow at the door. Do you want to come out?"

"Give us a minute."

They didn't need a minute before the door opened and the couple flew out sprinting toward the car. Isabel pressed the button to unlock the doors and they scrambled into the back seat. Isabel drove on, not knowing her destination, except away from the shadows that now pursued the car. Not wanting to exit the vehicle, the only choice seemed to be to leave the plantation altogether in hope that the shadows could not follow them beyond the perimeter of the property.

Isabel didn't see when the shadows disappeared, but she was gratified to mark their absence as she pulled onto the main road. Sarah and Michael, who had twisted around to see behind them now faced front. Michael was the first to break the silence.

"That's two nights in a row, which is two too many. Tonight's shadow visit was much more intense than last night. I'm not sure what we would have done if you hadn't come. I think we need to find a hotel, just to get a peaceful night's rest. Can you recommend somewhere?"

"Yes," she sighed, "Fulbright House is a nice little bed and breakfast; the Estate will pick up the tab for you." She prayed they would return the following day for the wedding. She now felt that something must be imminent, something that made her worry in a way she never had before. In all her years working on the Estate its reputation had never caused her concern; she had never felt anything that could be described as fear. Now she felt that the spirits were building toward some sort of climax.

"That's not necessary, Isabel," objected Michael, "we understand that you have no control over the situation."

"Frankly, I want to do it, especially if it means you'll return for the wedding tomorrow," she admitted. "Everything seems to be increasing in intensity and you seem to have a connection to whatever is happening that I do not. I feel like you're important in a way I can't explain."

"We'll come back in the morning, won't we Sarah?" Michael felt a momentary qualm since he had not consulted with her before issuing his reassurance. He was relieved to hear her agree.

"Of course, we will," agreed Sarah sounding more chipper than she really felt, "we've a got a wedding to attend."

Isabel pulled onto the shoulder of the road and got out her cell phone. She was relieved to be able to book a room for them on such short notice. This sort of thing had happened in the past when a frightened guest decided to pack their bags so she'd made an arrangement with Fulbright House which had served her well over the years. She planned to use discretionary funds she'd built into the budget to address situations such as this.

Soon the Daniels were all set in their new accommodations. Isabel had escorted them to their room and they asked her in to talk for a few minutes. Sarah had brought the note that was found in

Lynda's chiffonier and shared it with Isabel who examined it with interest.

"This is almost certainly Lydia's handwriting," Isabel said. "Of course, it would have to be identified as such by an expert, but I am confident that it's hers. The chiffonier is authentic to the estate and it was located in Lydia's bedroom, at least when I joined on. I suppose it could have been moved from a different spot, but it is an unwieldy piece of furniture and quite heavy to lift, even in two pieces."

"Why do you suppose it was never found?" asked Sarah.

"I guess we'll never know. I focused my search for documents in more obvious places so I'm not as upset to have missed this as I was the items found in *Jane Eyre*. It is interesting that the note is incomplete, yet never discarded. I imagine she might have been interrupted while writing it and never got a chance to finish it for whatever reason."

"I think the reason is that she died," said Michael.

"Well, it's late and I need to get some rest. I hope you'll be comfortable here. The Fulbright van will drive you back in the morning whenever you want to return."

"That's good," said Michael, "at least we won't have to explain to an Uber driver why Sarah is dressed and I'm in my pajamas."

Chapter 35

THE WEDDING DAY

Sarah and Michael sat on the wraparound porch at Fulbright House enjoying an unusually mild morning. The smell of bacon still hung in the air from the tasty breakfast spread they had enjoyed after a good night's rest. They were watching the antics of a small group of chickadees that were darting around the bird feeder that hung nearby.

"The birds are almost as fun to watch as a lot of what passes for entertainment on TV," remarked Michael as he finished off his cranberry juice.

"More, I'd say," said Sarah.

"Probably; how's your coffee?" asked Michael.

"Exceptionally good; how did you sleep last night?"

"Beautifully, and you?"

"Like a log."

"Ready to ask for a ride back? I'm looking forward to a change of clothes," said Michael who had added a robe provided by the inn to his ensemble.

"I suppose so," said Sarah. "Don't you think it's odd that we seem to keep needing a little respite from our vacation?"

"Yeah, next year let's just go to Disney World in July, it'll be relaxing."

Chapter 36

Isabel walked through the front hall mentally reviewing her wedding day checklist. She overheard snatches of a conversation between two guests as she passed.

"I had the strangest dream last night."

"Really? I barely slept at all. I had the feeling that something was wrong, but I couldn't put my finger on it."

In the kitchen, again hoping to snag a cup of coffee, she heard part of a phone call between an employee and guest.

"I'm so sorry that happened to you, we'll get your breakfast right out to you, sir."

"Good morning, Charles," Isabel addressed the employee, "What was the call about?"

"The folks in Pine Cottage said their sleep was disturbed last night. They were hearing noises like moaning but couldn't tell where it was coming from."

"Make sure they know that breakfast is on the house," she told him.

"That'll cheer them up," Charles smiled.

The kitchen manager briefed her on preparations for the wedding reception. The cake was being delivered later that morning and the ballroom looked beautiful. There appeared to be no last-minute fires to put out in terms of the menu. Isabel gratefully accepted a mug of coffee and started off for the ballroom to see it for herself. She purposely went into the lounge for a moment to see if guests were mingling there.

The parents of the groom were to be found sitting together at one of the small tables with their drinks. She stopped to greet them. Mrs. Stokes always seemed a little like a frightened bird to her, but this morning she was even more jumpy than she had seen her.

"Good morning," she said avoiding any platitudes about the "Big Day" since she was aware that there were difficulties.

"Morning," growled Mr. Stokes, omitting the adjective.

"I hope you'll let us know if there's anything you need," said Isabel since it was obvious that something was amiss.

"We *needed* to get a good night's rest last night, but that ship has sailed," he grumped.

"I'm so sorry, what seemed to be the issue?" asked Isabel who hoped she sounded more sincere than she was feeling.

"We *seemed* not to be able to sleep, because of the damn barking dog and some woman who was sobbing herself silly. I didn't know dogs were even allowed here and I couldn't figure out where the devil the crying was coming from."

"Guests are not permitted to bring pets and the stable dogs are trained to remain with the horses. We have never had any complaints regarding their barking, but I can look into it for you. Unfortunately, I am at a loss as to how to address the problem with the crying woman. If you experience problems again tonight, here is my direct number to call. I am sorry that your sleep was disturbed. I'll ask Isaac to comp your drinks." Isabel gave him her card. She had no intention of looking into the dogs; she had often heard complaints about "the barking dog" and had no answer for it. She usually tried to avoid giving out her direct number, but since this was the father-of-the-groom she would give him the V.I.P. treatment.

"If we 'experience problems again tonight' we'll just check out immediately and you can comp the final night of our stay," said Mr. Stokes unpleasantly.

"That is entirely up to you, sir. I do hope your day improves," said Isabel continuing on. She could readily see where the groom got his well-developed sense of entitlement. She stopped briefly for a word with Isaac before making her way to the ballroom.

There were no guests in the ballroom and after her encounter with Mr. Stokes, Isabel wished there was a reason to stay longer. Unfortunately, it looked perfectly ready to host a festive celebration. The tables were set, the dance floor polished, and the table arrangements were in place. The band would arrive later in the day and Katie would make sure they were settled. Next, she headed for the main hall to see how the canopy looked fully adorned with flowers.

Along the way she heard another guest commenting.

"Did you hear piano music late last night? I kept hearing it on and off. At first, I thought it was a radio, but it was awfully late and it seemed to be the same song every time it came on."

And another:

"Did you notice an odor last night? I kept checking the bottom of my shoes to see if I'd stepped in something."

Isabel noted each comment as she made her rounds. It could just be regular bad dreams and odd noises, but it seemed that few guests had slept well. She hoped the wedding couple had gotten some rest; she'd have to find a way to check on them.

The canopy looked beautiful covered in ivy and white roses and the main hall was fitted with chairs divided by a cloth aisle.

She knew everything would be in order, but it was her nature to check and double-check in an effort to eliminate any potential problems. She was grateful to finally arrive at her desk. She rang Magnolia Cottage to see if the Daniels had returned. No answer. Her coffee was waiting and she determined that she would take a few moments to enjoy it before looking at her emails. At least that was the plan until she noticed Katie in her doorway with a worried look on her face.

Chapter 37

M ichael changed into shorts and a polo shirt. He had an idea to ask Isabel about the Fairchild family burial plot. He knew it was located on the estate although he didn't see it on the map in the estate's brochure. He wasn't sure what Sarah would think of his idea so he thought it best to see if she had something she wanted to do before mentioning anything. He found Sarah lounging on the sofa paging through Isabel's record of reported disturbances.

"Spot anything interesting?" he asked.

"Not really. There's nothing in it that comes close to your weird, rainy visions. It's mostly sounds of moaning, music, and things that go bump in the night," she summarized in her characteristically concise manner.

The morning had passed pleasantly and without any unexpected premarital drama from Lynda. She hoped their luck would hold, although it felt a lot like waiting for the other shoe to drop. The wedding was scheduled for 7 p.m. so the rest of the day was wide open.

"What do you want to do today?" he asked Sarah.

"I haven't thought about it," she told him. "It's been such a nice, quiet morning."

"Don't jinx it," he warned. Sarah rolled her eyes at this.

"Maybe we could just hide in here today and take it easy," she suggested.

"We could; at least it doesn't turn into an evil shadow haven until after dark. By then we'll be at the wedding." He did his best to make 'evil shadow haven' sound appropriately sinister.

Sarah smiled at his attempt at humor. "I guess I was thinking of checking in on Lynda."

Michael resisted the urge to roll his eyes at this, but sighed and said, "Really, are you sure you want to do that?"

"Well, maybe just stop by. Joanna should be with her today, I know they have appointments with a hairdresser this afternoon. She told me the photographer is scheduled for four this afternoon to take some candid shots before the ceremony. From what she's told me Joanna wouldn't miss a photo op. If she's there I'll just say a quick hello and leave them to it."

"Okay, but I had a different idea."

"What is it?" asked Sarah.

"I remember that the obituary for Lydia Fairchild said she was buried on the estate, so I thought I'd ask Isabel if we could see the family burial plot," said Michael.

"Why?" asked Sarah simply.

"Oh, I don't know," he said, "it just seems like it might be interesting."

"Are you *trying* to have another vision? Remember, it didn't work with the pistols."

"No, of course not. I was wondering if James might be buried there, too. Maybe there's an unmarked grave."

"If her father didn't want Lydia to be courted by him, why on earth would he bury him in the family plot? It doesn't make sense," countered Sarah.

"Maybe it was easier to keep things quiet if they buried his body quickly. Isabel said the article was missing a lot of information and Colonel Fairchild seemed to have enough pull to keep the reporter from including more details. Maybe James isn't in the family plot itself, but nearby. I think it's worth a look." He was a little disappointed that she wasn't more enthusiastic.

"Isabel has a wedding to see to," she reminded him, "She may not have time for you today."

It was clear to Michael that Sarah had little interest in his idea. While she had been tending to the bride he had been largely left on his own. He had begun his inquiries in an effort to understand what was happening to him; now he was genuinely interested in unraveling the mystery surrounding Lydia's untimely death. Somehow the story felt unfinished and his opportunities to explore were dwindling.

"Well, it won't hurt to ask. I'll stop in at her office while you check on Lynda. Text me if she doesn't need you and we'll rendezvous."

"That'll work," said Sarah pleasantly enough. "I sure hope you're not turning into a ghost whisperer on me."

"Fine talk coming from the "bride whisperer," countered Michael.

Chapter 38

"Joanna Westmore checked out early this morning," said Katie.

Isabel closed her eyes. She was aware that this was her bride's maid of honor. She privately thought of her as a silly sort of woman, a party girl who, perhaps never grew up. The feisty redhead seemed an unlikely choice for the serious and practical bride.

When Lynda contacted her to ask about the availability of the venue for her wedding, she was delighted to be able to handle the arrangements for her friend. Well, if she was honest, they were more business associates than friends. Meeting up annually for the past four years at conferences and exchanging the occasional email hardly constituted a friendship. If she were even more honest, she'd admit that it didn't hurt when Lynda booked the full four-day package from Welcome Dinner to Wedding Reception. A stay at Southern Oak wasn't cheap, few brides could afford the complete luxury wedding package. In addition, her father paid the total cost of the rooms for those staying in the main house, which was mainly family and the bridal party members. She worried about how her bride was taking the news.

"She doesn't know yet," Katie informed her.

"She doesn't?"

"I don't think so. Jaquan was on last night and he said Ms. Westmore came to the front desk at about five this morning asking for her bags to be brought down. She was expecting an Uber to arrive to pick her up."

"I'll need to speak with Jaquan."

"He's waiting in the hall," said Katie.

Isabel was beginning to recover from the surprise and plan her response. She wasn't sure, at this point, that the four-day luxury package was worth all the trouble it was causing.

She was grateful for Katie who knew to give her a few minutes before breaking the news, and, who also knew that Jaquan would be the first person she would ask to see. She smiled an unspoken thank you to her assistant and asked her to send him in.

Jaquan appeared a little nervous to be asked to report to Miss Pennington. He worried that he may have handled the situation incorrectly. Isabel invited him to take a seat and tried to put him at ease. She needed to know more and wanted him to feel comfortable talking with her. He declined her offer of a choice of tea or a bottled water.

"So much fun working in customer service, isn't it?" she said smiling.

"Usually, it's alright," said Jaquan.

"Did our guest tell you anything about why she was leaving? Was she angry or upset?"

"She wasn't angry at first, more like scared. Her hands were shaking. I had to remind her about the no smoking policy, then she got mad."

"I see. What did she say?"

Jaquan hesitated before answering. He had heard the stories, but this was his first time fielding a problem with a guest who had been frightened enough to check out.

"Maybe I should have called you, ma'am," he said uncertainly, "but it was awfully early to wake you and I knew she wouldn't change her mind."

"It's alright, Jaquan, you haven't done anything wrong. It was a delicate situation. I just need to know what her complaint was."

"Well, uh, she said she saw a woman reflected in the window of her room, when she turned around there was no one there." Since all the bedrooms were located on the second floor and Joanna was not sharing a room with anyone, Isabel could understand why this had upset her.

"I see," said Isabel, "did she say anything else to you?"

"Yes ma'am, she said there was a message written in the frost of the window pane when she looked again."

"Frost? In July?"

"Yes ma'am, that's what she said."

"And what was this message?"

"'Til death us do part."

"Did anyone else see this message?"

"I asked Chris, after he finished with her luggage. He said he didn't see anything, but he wasn't looking for it. I went up to see for myself, there was nothing I could see." Jaquan seemed to be doubtful that it had ever been there.

"Thank you for coming up, Jaquan. I'm very glad you took the initiative to go up and look yourself, that bit of information is helpful," said Isabel ending the interview.

After her office cleared, she sat at her desk sipping her now cold coffee. She wondered if Joanna had left a note with some sort of explanation for Lynda. She looked at the time and decided she could safely ring her room, then hung up the phone when Katie reappeared in her doorway.

"Sorry to interrupt, but Mr. Daniels is here to see you."

Although his timing wasn't good, she agreed to see him. She was happy to know that he had returned after his experience last night.

"Good morning," said Michael, "is this a bad time? Your assistant practically winced when I asked to see you. I can come back later."

"No, it's fine I'm glad you're here. Sarah didn't come with you?" She was imagining Sarah refusing to leave Fulbright House in spite of her promise to come back.

"Sarah went up to see Lynda," said Michael.

"She did? Is she there now? Perhaps we could go up and join her; I have something to discuss with the bride and it might be helpful to have her there."

Michael did not expect this so he tabled his request for the moment. He could tell that something had set Isabel's day on its ear.

Chapter 39

Lynda answered her door pleasantly enough. Isabel apologized for the unannounced visit and asked if she could come in to discuss a "development". Lynda was surprised to see that she was accompanied by Michael.

Sarah caught his eye questioningly; he referred her to Isabel with a tilt of his head.

"What kind of 'development' brings you here?" asked Lynda, "Is Keith ...?

"This is not about Keith," Isabel quickly assured her. *Maybe I should have checked on Keith before seeing Isabel, too late now.*

"That's a relief," said Lynda, "so what's going on?"

"Have you heard from Joanna today?" asked Isabel. Both Lynda and Sarah sat up at the question. Sarah again tried to read Michael's expression, but he was avoiding her eyes.

"No, but she's not an early riser," smiled Lynda. "I don't expect to see her until we meet with the hairdresser."

"I'm sorry to tell you, but she checked out early this morning, around five a.m.; I don't think she's coming back. I was hoping she'd left you a note or something."

"She checked out? Without any explanation?"

All things considered Isabel thought she was taking the news pretty well. So far no tears, histrionics, or anger from this bride.

Keith's behavior had provided her ample opportunities to practice the art of remaining calm in the face of difficulties.

"She did mention something to the front desk clerk when she left. It's not the first time this has happened here at Southern Oak but she was *afraid* to stay. The clerk said she looked scared and she was shaking. I think I told you a little about the reputation the estate has for being haunted." Isabel thought it was convenient she and Lynda had discussed the topic in the past, although she knew Lynda was a skeptic.

"Did she say what scared her?"

"Yes, she saw a reflection of a young woman in her window; this type of thing has been reported in the past."

Michael and Sarah now made eye contact, but remained quiet allowing Isabel to lead the conversation. Lynda sat on the edge of the bed, looking thoughtful. Isabel decided not to mention the writing on the glass, at least for the moment. She was preoccupied with the idea that she should have checked on Keith first.

Lynda wasn't noticing her consternation; she was making up her mind.

"Sarah, if you would consider taking her place, it would make me very happy. I've been wishing I'd asked you in the first place."

"Of course I will," said Sarah after she recovered from the surprise, "but what will I wear?" she asked.

"I only have one attendant so there's really nothing to coordinate. Keith and Steve are both wearing a black tux, so you should be able to wear whatever you brought with you for the wedding. I loved what you had on last night; I expect you saved your best outfit for the ceremony so whatever it is, I feel like it will be just fine."

The two put their heads together planning to look at Sarah's dress to consider accessories. Michael felt a bit like a third wheel and he knew he'd see very little of her until after the wedding. He and Isabel took their leave.

"That went well," remarked Michael.

"It's about the only thing that has this morning," said Isabel as they walked down the hall together. "I'd like to knock on Mr. Stokes door to see if he needs anything."

Michael took a moment to put two and two together and realized she was talking about Keith. They stopped at a room at the end of the hall and he waited while she knocked. After the third try, she stopped knocking and suggested they return to her office.

"I never asked you why you stopped in to see me."

"I wanted to ask you if I could see the family burial plot; are guests allowed? I don't see it on the map in the brochure so maybe it's off limits?" He made his statement sound much like a question.

"It's actually part of the tours we do in October and November so it's not off-limits. We have not included it on the general brochure because it's quite a long walk, especially in the summer months. Of course it appears on the flyers we use for the tours. We walk with lanterns and I use a script I developed that retells a possible version of the story of the family scandal as we make our way to the gravesite. It's a popular activity with the locals. I can give you a copy of the brochure with directions. The path is up behind the stables." She pulled out a desk drawer and searched until she located one of the flyers and handed it to him.

"It looks like Sarah's day is planned so maybe I'll take a stroll," said Michael.

"It will be a hot walk. Are you sure you want to go alone?"

"Sure, why not?"

"Well, after the last two nights I wondered if ..."

Michael smiled, "It's broad daylight, what could happen?"

He sounded a little too flippant for Isabel. She felt he should know a little more about Joanna's departure.

"Mr. Daniels,"

"It's Michael, remember?"

"Michael, there's one thing Joanna said that I didn't mention to Lynda."

"Oh?'

"Yes, she said the woman left a message written on the glass of the window. She said it was written in the frost; I found that odd given the time of year." She waited to see how this was received.

"What was the message?"

"'Til death us do part."

"Like in a wedding ceremony?"

"Yes, of course we only have her word to the front desk clerk, but I can't imagine why anyone would make something like that up."

"You think it was meant for Joanna?"

"Well, she and Keith have been a bit – uh – flirty; maybe it was some kind of admonition." Isabel felt uncomfortable mentioning this to a third party. She had a strict rule about staying above conflicts among guests. She made a slight change of topic. "As I mentioned, it's been a rather bumpy morning. I've been hearing complaints as I circulate. Many of the guests are mentioning disturbances to their sleep last night. I really did want to check on Mr. Stokes this morning."

"Think the ghosts might have sent him a message, too?" asked Michael. "You know, yesterday Steve and I had a little chat with your Mr. Stokes. He and Lynda's dad had an argument and he was

AWOL for a while. Steve flat-out asked him if he was trying to hurt Lynda and he said something about being out-of-sorts and angry ever since he got here. Lynda told Sarah that he's been acting different, too. Makes me wonder if he is being affected by the resident spirits."

"Now I really do want to find him. Just to be sure he's okay," said Isabel rising from her desk.

"I'm going to take that stroll before the day gets any warmer," said Michael.

"Wait, take these," said Isabel reaching into the mini-fridge in the cabinet next to her desk. She handed him two bottles of water. "Will you let me know when you return?"

"Sure," said Michael feeling awkward with a bottle in each hand. He opened one, took a swig and added, "I'll drink to that!"

Chapter 40

Isabel began her search for Mr. Stokes at his parent's room. Remembering her earlier conversation with them she was almost relieved when no one came to the door. He wasn't in the lounge, nor had the valets brought out his car. She phoned room service to see if he had requested a meal and the front desk to see if they had any information for her. To save herself some footwork she sent out an email to all staff asking them to contact her if they saw Mr. Stokes, ostensibly to pass along a message. As a last resort she returned to his room and knocked once more. She was surprised when his mother came to the door.

"Yes?" said Mrs. Stokes.

"Good morning again, Mrs. Stokes," said Isabel thinking quickly, "I was hoping to speak with your son."

"He can't come to the door, he's uh, in the shower," she lied.

"Who is it?" came the voice of her husband.

"It's Miss Pennington, dear."

"Tell that woman it's not a good time."

"Uh," began Mrs. Stokes struggling to find words."

"I understand, please ask him to give me a ring when he is able. I won't need much of his time," said Isabel relieving her of the struggle in spite of her irritation at being designated 'that woman'.

"He can reach me any time at the same number I gave your husband earlier."

"I'll pass along the message," said Mrs. Stokes as she followed her into the hallway.

"Is there something else?" asked Isabel.

"Miss Pennington, I apologize for my husband's outburst this morning. We really were disturbed by a barking dog last night, but I don't know what he meant when he said her heard a woman crying. He kept getting up and listening at the wall and I when I said I couldn't hear it he got angry. Now, my son seems to be having some anxiety over the wedding."

"I'm very sorry to hear it," said Isabel. "Please ask Keith to call me, I may be able to help. Sometimes it's easier to talk to someone less familiar and I'm a very good listener."

Isabel left the Stokes family alone to decide if they wanted to take advantage of her offer to help. If they reached out she wasn't sure what she could do, but she would cross that bridge if she came to it. Of all the many weddings she had handled this one had presented more difficulties than any before. The groom had thrown several wrenches into the works, the maid-of-honor had abandoned the bride, even the best man had boycotted the rehearsal dinner. Now it was time to revisit the bride and her new attendant to see what problems they might present. Isabel had never had a wedding cancelled and wondered if this might be her first. Although she had done everything she could to prepare for a flawless ceremony and reception, she accepted that there were some things she could not hope to control. She took a moment to prepare before knocking gently at Lynda's door.

"Come in," called Lynda.

Sarah and Lynda were pleased with their progress toward an outfit for the maid-of-honor's stand-in. Sarah's dress was laid out on the bed. It was a simple tea-length, A-line style, sleeveless, with a V-neck in a lovely soft moss green. White sandals, pearls and a small clutch purse completed the ensemble.

"How nice," remarked Isabel, "looks like you have everything for your Matron of Honor."

"It was easy," said Lynda, "I love the color of her dress; we've just added my pearls to complete the outfit."

"And look," said Sarah, "I'm loaning Lynda my brooch. It looks perfect with her gown! Now she has something old and something borrowed from her "new" maid of honor." Sarah knew she was not *maid* of honor, but 'matron' sounded too old so she planned to ignore any use of the word when possible.

Isabel didn't note the change, she was more interested in the brooch.

"May I see it?" she asked.

"Of course," said Sarah, "Michael bought it at a nearby shop; it's got a connection to Southern Oak. The clerk told him it was authenticated as having belonged to Lydia Fairchild. Isn't it beautiful?"

"Sarah wore it last night and I was admiring it. When we went to her cottage to get her outfit, she offered it to me to use for the ceremony," added Lynda. "My gown has lace in a rose pattern and the carved roses on the pin complement it beautifully."

"How interesting that it once was worn by Lydia," said Isabel. She flipped it over to see the initials engraved on the back: L. F. She noted the similarity in their given names. "So, this piece has found its way home," she said handing it back to Lynda.

"At least until tomorrow," said Sarah.

Chapter 41

Michael finished the second bottle of water well before he reached the burial plot. He wanted to drink them while they were still cold. It was a mostly uphill climb in direct sun so he was grateful that the way back would at least be faster.

The family plot was well-maintained with a classic, short, white picket fence around the perimeter. Oak trees provided a shaded canopy and the temperature was noticeably cooler than the walk had been. As Michael expected, the view from the rise was exceptional. Behind him he could see the stables, riding paths and the roof of the main house. In front of him, low mountains were visible in the distance past lush, green, gently rolling hills that lay closer to his position.

Michael located Lydia Victoria Fairchild, Beloved Daughter next to her mother Virginia Stanton Fairchild, Devoted Wife and Mother. Colonel John Fairchild's grave looked peaceful enough in the bright summer sun. Several brothers and their wives were laid to rest as well as a few tiny graves of infants which caused Michael a moment of melancholy.

Outside of the family burial plot, and just over the crest of the hill, were a group of graves marked with simple crosses that bore only names and dates. A few only listed a first name; most carried only a single date, the date of death. These stones were much harder to read; they were not sheltered by trees and weather had eroded much of the writing. He found Livvy Pittman died 1869 and Eldin Pittman died 1871. Michael thought they must be the graves of the family's slaves. He wondered if one might belong to his friend Josiah, but could not locate his name.

One grave stood apart from the rest as though even the slaves would not include it among their number. Jes Warmad died 1865 was etched onto a small rectangular stone. Michael read the stone twice thinking it a strange sort of name. Warmad.

The heat was making its presence known and Michael climbed up the rise to where the family plot sat at the highest point with its impressive view in all directions. His plan to make quick work of the trek down to the main house was delayed when he saw someone kneeling in front of Lydia's marker. He was clearing some of the weeds that encroached upon her resting place.

"So, you tend to this area as well as the gardens," stated Michael to Josiah.

"Yes, suh."

"I thought you preferred to work in the mornings and evenings."

"It's not so bad under the trees."

"Josiah, where are you, when you aren't here?" asked Michael.

"I'm at peace."

"Then why come back?"

"I'm drawn to this place."

"What draws you here?"

"I could always ease Miz Lyddie's sorrow, she needs me now, so I come."

"How do you help her?"

"I 'jus be with her, it's all I kin do."

"It's kind of you to give up your peace for her."

Josiah shrugged at this. "Her daddy took her peace; he wuz angry 'til the day he died. Miz Lyddie died too sad. The past is done, can't change nuthin'".

Michael heard a soft bark and turned to see that the dog was also in attendance.

"Does the dog soothe Miss Lyddie too?"

Josiah smiled a little. "Miz Lyddie loved dogs and hosses. She could make friends with the meanest cur. She had this 'un rollin' on hiz back for a belly rub in no time." The dog's tail wagged slowly as if in agreement.

All of Michael's visits with Josiah had been brief, so he knew he needed to make good use of the time he had. He could ask about the changes in Keith but decided against it. Keith was not of Josiah's time.

"There's a grave beyond the rise that doesn't seem to belong," said Michael.

Josiah made no reply, he continued to tug at a stubborn weed. Michael took the hint and abandoned the topic. He was beginning to feel the heat and knew he should begin to head back soon. He hesitated, feeling that this might be his last conversation with the old gentleman.

"Tonight is the wedding and tomorrow I'll be heading back home. I'll miss talking with you Josiah."

"Don't be gitin' ahead of yourself," warned Josiah.

"Ahead of myself?"

"Not time to be sayin' goodbye."

There was a subtle change in Josiah. He was avoiding looking in Michael's direction, focusing intently on the weeds around Lydia's gravesite as if each weed removed could ease her suffering.

"You needs to do what you been doin', suh. I don't know what that is, but it helps 'em both. You'll need to help them or -" Josiah broke off, his head turning left and right.

"Josiah?"

The dog barked softly behind him and Michael turned to look. The dog met his eyes and sat, his tail wagging slowly, a good boy. Michael knew in that moment that Josiah had gone. Perhaps he had gone back to his place of peace, perhaps his mistress needed him elsewhere. Wiping the sweat from his brow, he began the downhill trek toward the manor.

Chapter 42

I sabel sat at her desk feeling uneasy about the day. Complaints from guests were more numerous than usual but the staff were able to handle most of the issues. Keith had not reached out to her and Michael had not returned. Only the bride and Sarah seemed to be enjoying their morning together.

She was unaccustomed to feeling so much concern on the day of a main event. She had reviewed her checklist and knew that everything was in place. The kitchen staff would begin to arrive soon to begin food prep, the band was due to arrive at around 5 p.m. and Katie was prepared to handle them. The main issue at the moment was the anxious groom. She wondered if the best man would return, perhaps he could talk to Keith. Since he was not a registered guest she had no way to contact him. She picked up her desk phone and punched in four numbers.

"Hello, Miss Fuller, this is Isabel. I was wondering if you have had any word from Keith's best man. I think his name is Steve."

"No, I haven't but I have a number for him. Shall I ask him to contact you?"

"Yes, I would appreciate it if you could."

"May I ask why?"

"There is some concern, after last night, that he may not return for the ceremony," said Isabel, "I would feel better to know this ahead of time if possible. The wedding could continue without him, but we would need another witness for the marriage certificate."

"I see, I'll text him your number and ask him to get in touch right away," said Lynda, "I don't think you need to worry though. I think we convinced him to come last night."

"Oh, that is good to hear. I would still like to confirm it with him if possible."

"I'll do it right now."

"Thanks so much."

Isabel hung up the phone and began to prepare tea. At least it was something to do until she heard from Steve, or Keith, or Michael. Apparently neither Keith nor his parents had reached out to Lynda to alert her to Keith's anxiety. This made her wonder if she was worrying over nothing. Her mind hopped to Michael. Where was he? She thought he should be back from his visit to the cemetery. If he wasn't back by the time she finished her tea she would take a cart and drive up there to look for him. In the meantime she checked her emails, she could always occupy herself productively with emails.

Most of the emails were about the next event on the calendar. Next week was a family reunion. As usual the family would begin to arrive on Wednesday afternoon and stay through the following Monday morning. A bit longer than a wedding, but much less fuss. She should be able to take both Monday and Tuesday off, a thought that had more than the usual appeal.

Her cell phone buzzed and she answered. It was Steve and yes, he was coming. He planned to arrive around 5 p.m. for some early photographs.

"Is it possible for you to come sooner?"

"How much sooner?"

"Well, as soon as you are able. There is an issue you may be able to help us with. I'd prefer to talk in person," said Isabel. She was walking a fine line in terms of breaking a confidence, until he was here she felt better saying as little as possible.

"I can get my things together and be there in an hour," replied Steve.

"I can't thank you enough. You'll find me in my office." She ended the call happy to know that the best man was still on board. Three-quarters of the wedding party were confirmed. One to go.

Katie appeared in her doorway with Michael who looked a little worse after his excursion. Isabel nodded to Katie who smiled and departed. She reached into the mini fridge for a bottle of water and motioned to a chair. Michael happily took a seat and the bottle of water, downing it immediately.

"Would you like another?"

"Yes, please," said a grateful Michael.

"How was your visit?" asked Isabel.

"It's beautiful up there, almost worth the heat stroke," he said with a smile.

"I did warn you."

"I wanted to ask you about one of the graves. It was for someone named Jes Warmad, Jess with just one ess."

"Jes Warmad? Are you sure that was the name?"

"Yes, positive. It isn't part of the family plot and it's even set apart from the other graves that are there just down the slope."

"Oh yes, I know what you're talking about now. I just didn't know the name on the stone. Jes Warmad you say?"

"It's an unusual name isn't it? Do you know any more about who it is?"

"No, most folks don't even notice it. I always thought they were just opening up a new section," said Isabel, "such an odd name."

"I asked Josiah about it and he ignored my question," Michael told her.

"Josiah was there? I'm surprised you didn't lead with that. Did he have a message for you today?"

"He told me to 'keep doing what I'm doing'. Too bad I have no idea what it is I've been doing," said Michael. "He wouldn't let me say goodbye to him though."

"Why were you saying goodbye?"

"Because I'm leaving tomorrow and I probably won't see him again," said Michael as if it should be obvious.

"Of course," said Isabel feeling like she was a step behind. "How did he stop you from saying it?"

"He told me not to get ahead of myself, it wasn't time, I need to help them *both*. It's kind of confusing really."

"What was that name on the gravestone again?" asked Isabel.

"Jes Warmad." He spelled it for her.

Isabel sat at her desk. She picked up a pen and wrote Jes Warmad on the pad next to the phone. Michael had surprised her with his mention of the grave that was set apart. She thought she knew everything about Southern Oak. How many tours had she hosted tours up to the family cemetery over the years and yet not noted the name on the stone?

"It sounds made up. I've never heard of anyone related to Southern Oak with the surname of Warmad," remarked Isabel.

The copy of *Jane Eyre* was on the corner of her desk. She reached for it and opened it to the page with Lydia's tiny handwriting experimenting with a new name for herself, Mrs. James Alden Ward. Michael looked over her shoulder.

"Ward and Warmad, hmmm," he said the names aloud.

"A bit similar, aren't they? Too bad it wasn't James instead of Jes," said Isabel.

"If you remove the middle name, both have nine letters," pointed out Michael.

Isabel wrote: James Ward. Jes Warmad. At last she saw it. She crossed out the a and m in James and wrote m and a over the name Ward.

"They are anagrams!" said Isabel.

Had Michael found the grave of Lydia's soldier?

Chapter 43

M ichael returned to the cottage for a much-needed shower. It was still too early to dress for the evening so he slipped on a pair of khakis and a fresh t-shirt. He was excited to share his discovery with Sarah so he texted to see if she wanted to meet up for lunch. Ah, she and Lynda had plans, of course they did. No dear, that's fine, have a good time. It could wait. Now that he had cooled off he realized how hungry he was and ordered a club sandwich from room service. While he waited he flipped on the television and cruised until he settled on an old western. He was a little annoyed to find himself alone watching TV on his vacation while Sarah made herself a member of the bridal party. Would she now be seated at the head table while he sat with strangers at the reception? He would have to do something about that. Sarah would call him "hangry" if she were here. He walked over to the minifridge and selected a candy bar and a can of soda. He had just finished the last tasty bite when his food arrived. Oh what the heck, dessert first is okay when on vacation.

The movie really wasn't very good and the food made him drowsy. When he caught himself beginning to nod off he resisted the urge. He was determined not to spend his day as a couch potato dozing in the glow of the TV set. He roused himself and grabbed his fishing rod, tackle box, and a bottle of water. The lake beckoned and he would answer the call.

The boat was available at the dock but Michael wasn't really a boat guy. He usually fished in the surf on the Gulf of Mexico, so fresh water fishing was a novel experience. He scouted out a good spot and cast his line into the lake near some grasses where he thought the fish might hide. He had heard that the lake was stocked with trout and that the kitchen would even cook up your catch. Michael might have taken them up on the offer except that he knew they were busy with the wedding banquet. Lucky for the trout; he caught and released four nice sized specimens thinking that it was good that Sarah was occupied elsewhere. He never seemed to tire when he fished in the gulf where he could wade out up to his hips; standing on the shore was a slightly different story. After an hour or so he walked to one of the benches near the lake to take in the view. Fishing relaxed him like little else; he loved being outdoors around the water.

His peaceful afternoon was interrupted when he felt that there was someone behind him. He turned to look and saw Keith stop abruptly as if he might turn back the way he came. Michael was relieved it was an actual living person, then he looked more carefully and saw that Keith looked nervous and upset. He sighed, knowing that his peaceful interlude had come to its end.

"Hot one, isn't it?" he said smiling as if he hadn't noticed anything amiss.

Keith looked startled and seemed at a loss as to how to respond. Michael tried again.

"I've had some luck fishing, the trout seem to love my lures. Threw 'em all back, though."

Keith still did not respond but approached and sat next to Michael. They sat quietly for a few minutes before Michael tried again, this time addressing Keith's apparent difficulty.

"So, a bit nervous on the big day?" he asked.

"More than a bit," Keith replied.

"I'm sorry to hear that. Trouble in paradise?"

"Not exactly."

"I know I was a bundle of nerves on my wedding day," offered Michael. It wasn't true, but he was trying to connect in some way. He hoped to get him talking.

"I saw something, or, some*one*."

"Who?" Michael was afraid he knew where this was heading.

"I don't know. I've seen him a few times; he would be there and then just gone. I shrugged it off at first, but it keeps happening. This morning – I know this sounds crazy -" Keith did not go on. Michael was practically a stranger to him, but maybe that would be easier. He hadn't been able to tell his parents. He just told them he hadn't slept well, which was true enough; and was a little nervous, which was an understatement. Then his dad went off on how he'd heard a dog barking and some lady crying all night and turned the conversation back to himself. Typical.

"I've had some weird experiences here myself," said Michael. "It's why I was so shook up at the Welcome Reception that first night and again at your rehearsal." Keith looked at him as if seeing him for the first time.

"What did you see?"

"You wouldn't believe me if I told you."

"Try me."

"I saw a young woman playing a piano, she seemed sad," Michael told him. "Then I saw a soldier. They were there and then gone." He kept his descriptions deliberately brief.

"Shit, I didn't know, man," said Keith, "I've been such an ass."

"How could you know? Anyway, you were just joking around," said Michael.

"No, I've been an ass. I'm ruining everything and *he knows it*," said Keith miserably.

"Who knows it?"

"The- the- man I keep seeing knows. He said he would not stand for any marriage to take place. He was deadly serious and then he just wasn't there. I think I'm losing my mind. I think I have to call it off."

"Call it off? Why?" asked Michael, now worried.

"Because I've been unfaithful and he knows it; I have to tell her."

"How were you unfaithful?"

"Joanna."

"Seriously? How did you know Joanna? I thought she was a friend of Lynda's from college or something."

"I didn't know her before, but we just clicked. Shit, this is a mess."

"Joanna is gone, she checked out today," Michael told him. "Did you really -?"

"Well no, not *really* in the sense that we acted on anything more than sneaking kisses together. What do you mean she checked out?"

"The desk clerk said she was 'afraid to stay,'" said Michael making little two-finger quote signs in the air. "She was shaking and upset; she called an Uber and left."

"Afraid to stay?"

"That's what he said, or words to that effect. I didn't talk to him, Isabel did."

"I don't know what to do."

"Before you do anything why not talk to Isabel? She can help you decide how to tell Lynda. Then she can advise you both on how to handle telling your guests. Or maybe call Steve, ask him what he thinks?" Michael was grasping for any suggestion Keith might seize on. He imagined poor Lynda's disappointment. He had an urge to call Sarah and give her a heads up.

"I think Steve's done with me," said Keith.

Michael felt badly about his role in Steve's early departure the previous evening.

"I don't think so," he said encouragingly. "C'mon, you can't just sit here, the longer you wait the harder it will be on Lynda and she doesn't deserve this."

"How do I find Isabel?" asked Keith.

"Let's try her office."

They walked together toward the main house not speaking. Keith was subdued but Michael thought he seemed calmer. As they got nearer Michael saw a familiar figure pruning some plants in the garden. Michael caught his eye and Josiah nodded approvingly as they climbed the steps toward the main entrance.

Chapter 44

Isabel hung up the phone. The kitchen manager called to let her know that the cake had arrived in good condition. The photographer would arrive next. He was to meet with the bride for photos at four and with the groom at five. Lynda and Sarah were with the hairdresser and things were progressing according to schedule.

Katie appeared in the doorway with Steve. Isabel thanked him for coming and asked him to come in and have a seat. She closed the door to allow some privacy and hoped she could explain the situation in a way that would not make her seem to be meddling.

"Your call was the last thing I expected," said Steve.

"I'm sure," agreed Isabel, "there is a situation brewing with the groom. I don't have specifics. His parents mentioned that he was having some anxiety, more than the usual wedding day jitters. I was hoping you might be able to help in some way."

"Where is he?" asked Steve.

"He was in his room with his parents, but they said he left to take a walk."

"Yesterday he seemed angry and then I heard he apologized to Lynda and things were back on track. Today he's anxious?"

"Yes, according to his parents. I haven't talked with him personally. I thought he might have reached out to you."

"I'm sorry, but he hasn't."

Isabel closed her eyes to think when she heard a soft knock on the door. Katie's knock.

She opened the door to find Katie with Michael. Isabel was just about to explain that she would not have time for him when she saw Keith standing behind him. She invited them both in and asked Katie to limit interruptions. She also asked her to pick up her calls until her meeting with the groom had concluded. One look at Keith and she knew her worst fears were likely confirmed.

"Keith, I'm glad to see you. How can I help?"

Once Keith began talking, he went on for quite a while. Isabel had planned to ask him if he wanted to talk to her alone, but it didn't seem to matter to him. He had met Joanna at the mixer before the Welcome Dinner, it wasn't her fault, he didn't identify himself as the groom at first. They discovered a mutual interest in adventure vacations. Both had gone zip lining over the rainforest in Costa Rica with magnificent views, a once in a lifetime experience. This led to comparing other adventure trips including hot air ballooning and white-water rafting. Joanna was pretty, vivacious and fun-loving. At one point Joanna pulled him aside and snuck a quick kiss. Of course, once the dinner began his secret was out. Joanna found the revelation amusing and continued to flirt all through the evening. She was clever about it and Lynda, seated right beside her, never suspected a thing. Later that night, after the meal was long over, he searched her out to apologize. She told him not to worry and agreed that the timing was terrible, and wasn't it too bad. It wouldn't happen again. But it did, twice the following day, just briefly, never sharing more than a kiss. Keith swore he had never been unfaithful to Lynda before.

The second night Keith began to see him. At first it was just a glimpse out of the corner of his eye, something he could easily dismiss. The man was tall, with dark piercing brown eyes. His hair was just turning gray with a salt and pepper look. He wore a white shirt open at the neck. It wasn't until he came into his dreams that Keith realized the depth of his anger. In his dream the man held a gun pointed at him. His look was undeniably murderous. Sightings during the daytime were no longer brief glimpses. His guilt kept him from sharing anything about his visions with Lynda. Last night was the worst of all, he didn't dare sleep and see him in his dreams. He paced his room, expecting to see him at any moment. He felt that the man knew of his infidelity and was punishing him. He heard a voice but didn't see anyone. It was strident, authoritative; furious. It kept repeating: 'I will not allow such a marriage to take place'. He said it over and over. Finally in desperation Keith went to his parents' room.

"I don't know what to do," he concluded.

"It's just like last night, Keith, you need to talk to Lynda, but this time give her the whole story, just as you've told us," said Michael.

"I apologized," said Keith.

"But she doesn't know what you were really apologizing for; because it's not for inviting extra guests or hiring a band, is it?" Michael asked.

"If I do. she'll call it off," said Keith.

"Time is short, we need to find out," said Isabel.

She was determined to save the bride from an embarrassing public scene. She phoned Lynda's room and was relieved when she answered on the first ring. They arranged to meet in Isabel's office. She asked Steve and Michael to wait in the nearby library in case she needed them. Lynda arrived wearing jeans and a white cotton blouse, but with her hair in an elegant braided updo with pearl accents. Lynda knew something was wrong before she arrived, when she saw Keith her heart sunk. Isabel sat behind her desk while they talked. She could have left the room, but unless they asked her to leave, she wanted to stay to hear exactly how much Keith told her. She needed to know as soon as possible if the wedding would be going forward or not.

Sarah arrived a few minutes after Lynda looking a little lost. Katie directed her to the library where she found Michael and Steve waiting nervously. Like Lynda she was dressed casually but with her hair in a stylish French twist with baby's breath accents. Michael explained the situation to her.

"Poor Lynda," said Sarah sadly, "I think she was just beginning to relax and have some fun today."

"Well, it explains why her bridesmaid was never around," said Michael.

"I wonder what actually happened to frighten her into checking out," said Sarah.

Steve had been quiet since hearing Keith's account of seeing visions of some mysterious man. He worried that his college friend was losing his grip on reality, but the reactions of Isabel and Michael puzzled him. They both seemed to accept it as true, even reasonable. Michael was realizing that Steve was hearing about visions for the first time.

"Isabel didn't tell her everything earlier, we know a little more about what scared Joanna."

"Pray tell," said Sarah who never liked pregnant pauses.

"She saw a message written on the window in her room. It looked to be written in frost. It said "'til death us do part."

"Like in an old-fashioned wedding vow?" asked Steve who was still processing.

"Yes, the plantation has a reputation for being haunted. People often report seeing and hearing odd things, much like what Keith described. Isabel even does a haunted tour around Halloween," explained Michael.

"And it's not the first time guests have checked out because of something they've seen," added Sarah.

"Sounds like you both think the place is haunted," observed Steve.

"I do," said both Michael and Sarah together and then chuckled.

"It might explain Keith's behavior, at least some of it," said Steve.

"Some of it, maybe," said Sarah doubtfully.

Steve and Michael looked at her questioningly.

"Well, he had to have hired the band before he arrived. It's hard to book a band at the last minute. And I bet he invited the extra guests before he got here, too," said Sarah.

"I know that he meant the band to be a welcome surprise," said Steve diplomatically, "he sat and chose the music for the DJ with her just so she wouldn't suspect anything."

"Well, it was a surprise alright," said Michael.

"And the extra guests were to correct an error he'd made. His mom was furious when they realized he'd only given a partial list to Lynda. He found the extra page of names in his car when he had it detailed for the wedding trip. I don't know if he ever fully explained the situation to Lynda."

"I guess you never really know what someone is dealing with," said Sarah, "but I sure would love to hear their conversation."

Chapter 45

The Main Hall looked exquisite. Roses and baby's breath arrangements adorned the chairs on the aisle leading up to the canopy that was bedecked in such a way that it looked as though the flowers had grown there naturally. A string quartet, a surprise gift from Lynda's father, sat quietly waiting for a signal to begin from Isabel. Guests were arriving and getting settled; a soft murmur of anticipation could be heard around the room.

Michael was seated in the second row on the bride's side. He assumed this was because of Sarah's new role as a member of the bridal party. He had been stunned when he heard that the ceremony would go on as planned. Perhaps Lynda felt pressure to carry on given that the guests were already assembled and some had traveled far to be there. He thought it improbable that she had no misgivings whatsoever. How different this was from his own wedding. He and Sarah had married in a small church wedding with about the same number of guests and a simple reception in the parish hall. There were no on-site appointments for manicures and hairdressers and certainly no string quartet. What they did have, however, was joy and an aura of celebration void of any of the sort of ego or drama that had characterized this event.

Steve walked down the aisle and seated first the mother of the bride, and soon after, the mother of the groom and her husband.

He then took his place beside the groom at the canopy. The string quartet began to play Pachelbel's Canon in D and the guests were directed to rise as the matron of honor began her walk down the aisle. Michael caught Sarah's eye as she passed, she smiled back at him; he knew they were both thinking back to their own nuptials. The bride followed, looking lovely escorted down the aisle by her father who managed to look proud, although not especially happy.

The music came to an end and Lynda's father gave her a quick kiss and returned to his seat wiping a single tear. Lynda joined Keith at the canopy. The officiant asked everyone to be seated. There were chairs for the bridal party on either side of the canopy. Steve and Sarah to her right and the bride and groom to her left.

Michael was pleased when Reverend Vaughan was true to her word and kept her remarks relatively brief. She included some light-hearted humor at the outset but ended on a more serious note talking about a lifetime of dedication to one another. Michael was listening, but began to be distracted by an unpleasant odor, it took him only a moment to identify the earthy aroma of - manure? He looked around and saw other noses near him begin to wrinkle. Reverend Vaughan ended her remarks and asked the bridal party to stand. Lynda handed her bouquet to Sarah.

Reverend Vaughan began, "Dearly beloved, we are gathered here today in the presence of God and these witnesses to join Keith Emerson Stokes and Lynda Veronica Fuller in holy matrimony, which is an honorable estate, instituted of God. Therefore, it is not to be entered into unadvisedly, but reverently and soberly. Into this holy estate, these two persons present come to be joined. Therefore, if anyone can show just cause why they may not be lawfully joined together, let them speak now or forever hold their peace."

Michael felt the first drops as he rose from his seat. Rain; the first slow droplets of a summer shower. He could not believe this was happening again. He looked at Sarah expecting her to begin to fade from his sight. He began to steel himself for the wave of emotions and tried to remember the locket, the note from James, and the unfinished note from Lydia. But Sarah did not fade, nor did any of the other guests. He saw them stir and brush away raindrops just as he had. He found himself unable to move from his position just as in his other visions. And the rain began to fall in earnest.

Other things faded, the canopy, the chandeliers, and a piano in the far corner of the room were gone. Only the people remained and the smell of horses and a stable.

First to appear was Lydia, standing near one of the stalls feeding an apple to one of the horses. There was the roll of thunder and the sound of rain falling heavily. James came next, sitting on a low stool not far from her, his hat in his hands. The emotion that filled the room was one of melancholy. Lydia turned to James, the apple forgotten, and looked at him with eyes that begged him to stay. The mood changed radically when John Fairchild's figure filled the doorway full of fury and carrying the pearl handled pistol. None of the three looked at Michael as they had in his earlier visions. This felt more like watching the climactic scene of a tragedy unfold before him.

It happened in the blink of an eye. James jumped to his feet, John raised his gun, Lydia saw it and hurried to James to shield him. The bullet grazed her side and hit James in his stomach. Michael saw the now familiar wound, the blood staining his shirt, the look of shock and outrage on his face. He saw John bury his face in his hands as he realized the enormity of his actions. New to the scene was Lydia lying on the ground near James holding her side, crying, her blood beginning to stain her dress. Michael felt her surprise, her loss, her sense of confusion, her grief. She exuded no anger, as if it simply was not in her nature.

The scene ended. The rain eased, slowed, then stopped. Michael waited to feel the pulling sensation and dizziness that signaled the end of a vision, but it did not come. Like a patron of the theatre he watched the scene change. Now there was a bedroom where Lydia was attended to by her aunt and another woman he did not know. She appeared to be in a fever. They pulled back the cover and lifted her garment to change the bandage on the wound in her side. Michael could see that it was badly infected. John Fairchild came to the doorway; somehow he seemed not to fill the space as he had before. He sat on the chair next to her bed in an attitude of prayer. Michael was overwhelmed by John's sense of guilt and grief.

Now, at last, came the pulling sensation and welcome dizziness. The room righted itself around him. The chairs, flowers, light fixtures and canopy returned, solid and reassuring. People near him began to stir, a few collapsed. Michael searched for Sarah who looked unsteady and was being assisted by Steve. Keith was on his knees, visibly shaken. Lynda had managed to find her chair and sat calmly, as if waiting for the next act.

The people around him were quiet at first, but soon they began to talk in excited whispers. Michael saw Isabel walking haltingly through the room, checking on guests as she came. Almost everyone was now seated, most unable to get back on their feet. He knew the feeling all too well. He wondered how many of them would want to check out early as Joanna had.

Soon Michael felt steady enough and began to make his way to Sarah.

"Jesus, Michael, is this what your visions have been like?" she asked him.

"Not all of them," said Michael, "this one was pretty intense."

"That was unreal," said Steve.

"I'm glad it's over," said Sarah.

Michael looked over her shoulder and whispered, "I don't think it is."

Michael was perhaps the first to see the form of John Fairchild materialize beside Keith who cowered below him still on his knees. His clothing was no longer worn and he looked more like the man he once was.

"You are too easily led astray," John's eyes locked on Keith as his voice filled the room, "This marriage will not stand."

Sarah gasped as she saw Lydia appear next to Lynda, each wearing the same rose brooch. Lydia, too, looked like she had in life. She wore the same dress that Michael remembered from his first vision of her at the piano. The two women met as kindred spirits; somehow there was an understanding between them.

John's eyes were gentle as they rested on Lydia. "My beloved daughter, can you forgive me the harm I've done? My stubborn hatred and prejudice kept you from having love, stole your very life," John's voice broke.

"Father, I forgive you. I know how you grieved over every lost soldier. The war affected your attitudes. I always felt loved by you, even when we disagreed," she told him.

James was the final spirit to emerge. Without his visage contorted in anguish he was a handsome young man. He stood between Steve and Michael, his steel gray eyes softened when they found Lydia.

John spoke now to James. "I wronged you in life. I simply could not find it in my heart to bless your union to my daughter. Would that I could amend my grievous transgression."

"Why can't you?" asked Michael who was shocked to hear the sound of his own voice. When no one replied he continued. "Here we are in this wonderful old house, all dressed up for a wedding. Maybe there should be a wedding. James and Lydia's love has survived death, surely they deserve to be united in matrimony. What do you think, John?"

"I would now bless their union," said John.

"But how can it be done?" asked Sarah.

"We would need hosts, we cannot remain long without them," said Lydia looking at Lynda who understood and smiled.

"Who will host James?" asked Michael.

"If Lynda doesn't mind, I think I could do it," said Steve.

"Oh, I don't mind at all," Lynda assured him.

"What is happening?! What are you people doing?" cried an incredulous Keith at last rising clumsily to his feet.

Lynda answered calmly, "We want to help them."

"You can't do this!" exclaimed Keith, "I won't be a part of it!"

Keith's parents went to him, as did Reverend Vaughan. She spoke softly to him for a moment, but he was having none of it. He fled the room, his parents in tow with Reverend Vaughan looking on with concern.

Isabel slipped seamlessly back into her role as event planner. She crossed the room to intercept the good reverend.

"I wonder if I might have a word," said Isabel.

"Certainly," said the minister.

"I understand that you may want to be with the Stokes family," she began.

"No," the Reverend cut her off, "they need a bit of time before they will be able to revisit what they have seen."

"And you?" asked Isabel.

"I am in awe," admitted Reverend Vaughan.

"I wonder if you might consider presiding over this unorthodox ceremony? They very much want to marry. I think it would be healing for them."

"If they will have me, I would be honored."

Isabel went to the front of the canopy.

"I have an announcement," she said. "If everyone is in agreement, in a few moments we will begin again." Here she paused to allow the new wedding party time to consider. When no objections arose, she continued. "If you would like to stay to witness the marriage of Lydia Victoria Fairchild and James Alden Ward please return to your seats. If you prefer to leave you may do so at this time."

A handful of people had already departed with the Stokes family. No one else left the room. There was an excited murmur from the guests as they reseated themselves.

Michael spoke up, "What about John? Surely he wants to escort his daughter down the aisle. Doesn't he need a host?"

"He does," said Isabel, "Are you volunteering?"

"I, uh, Sarah?" Michael knew this was not a decision he should make unilaterally.

"Is this what you want to do, Michael?" asked Sarah.

"I think so, yes," said Michael.

"Everyone to their places," directed Isabel, "Sarah, you, John and the bride go to the rear of the room and wait for the music.

James, you stand there." She pointed to the position to the left of Reverend Vaughan who was already in place. "Let me know when you are ready."

Isabel watched the transformation of Lynda into Lydia. Lydia on her own was translucent; then she simply stepped into the space that was Lynda. For a moment she could see both visages, then Lynda's outline became translucent for an instant before vanishing altogether. It was surreal. Sarah, as matron of honor, stood beside her in awe. By the time Isabel turned her attention to the canopy, the groom and his father stood transformed.

There was a nervous flutter from the guests as they became aware of shadows forming at the edges of the room. The shadows drew inward toward the gathering. As they drew closer, they became more defined as individuals who hovered lovingly rather than menacingly around the gathering. Isabel cued the musicians and the ceremony began.

The ceremony had an ethereal quality, as if a dream. Lydia and John glided down the aisle toward James. The Reverend welcomed everyone briefly and began the rite without a homily. Lydia' father now, not only approved the union, but also acted as James' best man. Vows were exchanged, tears of joy were shed, and finally, a kiss.

The kiss began as James and Lydia, but ended as Steve and Lynda. The transformation could not last, but the happy couple remained a few moments before fading forever from view. Steve and Lynda ended their kiss shyly, both blushing vividly and ending with happy smiles. The shadows departed as swiftly as they had come.

Chapter 46

The reception was nothing short of glorious. Keith had made an excellent decision with his choice of a band and they played unaware of the events that had transpired in the main hall. The photographer, who knew what had come before, simply circulated the room getting candid photos of the party-goers mingling, dining and on the dance floor.

Kitchen staff and servers were only told that the wedding was off, even though most of them would swear that they heard music and voices that certainly sounded like a wedding took place. The reception would go on as planned; no sense wasting all that food with so many hungry guests still in evidence. They were further confused when there were, indeed, toasts to the happy couple. The catering manager asked if the cake should be served in light of developments and was given the go-ahead. He later remarked that for a broken engagement, it was the most festive celebration he had worked in recent memory.

Michael and Sarah laughed, ate, toasted and danced the night away.

"You did good, husband," Sarah told Michael.

"I did, didn't I?"

"What was it like?"

"I don't really remember much. After all this I kind of missed the wedding!"

"I'll tell you all about it later, dear."

"Lynda and Steve look like they are having a good time," observed Michael.

"I told you."

"Yes, you did."

Chapter 47

SUNDAY

Michael rose early and dressed. He kissed Sarah and told her he was going for one last stroll on the grounds. Sarah mumbled something about it being too early and rolled over pulling the covers with her.

It was a very pretty morning, blue skies, not too warm yet and he was enjoying the birdsong as he walked toward the carriage house. Phoebe was there, she was in a good mood because it would be a short day for her; she should be home by noon.

"Good morning, Mr. Daniels," she greeted him, "Are you ready to check out?"

"No, not quite yet," he said, "the missus is still resting."

"How can I help you?"

"I was looking for information about booking a reservation in the future. It's such pretty part of the country; it might be nice to see it in the fall."

"Oh, you should, it's truly lovely here in the fall, cool days and changing colors," she told him, "I have some information right here. Think you might be interested in one of our ghost tours?"

Michael smiled, "Why not? Everyone loves a good ghost story."

He pocketed the flyer and walked toward the gardens. Josiah had not allowed him to say goodbye and he had not been in attendance at the wedding. He was disappointed not to see him tending to the flowers. It was still early enough to walk up to the stables and say farewell to the horses, at least they should be available for a visit.

The horses did not disappoint. They allowed a nice scratch behind the ears and responded to his whinnies and snorts. The smell of the stable brought back memories of the previous evening. He wished he could remember more about it, but Sarah would fill him in on the drive home. After a visit with each of the horses he sighed and turned toward the stable doors.

Josiah was there, talking softly to the mare in the first stall. The dog stood next to him his tail wagging slowly.

"I didn't think I'd see you again."

"That's why I came. You did good, son," said Josiah.

"Why weren't you there last night?"

"Not my place to be, wouldn't be right."

"It would be your place nowadays."

"Mebbe. My place is with the flowers, the lake, the hosses."

"Will you go now?"

"I'm at peace now like I never wuz."

"And what about you, fella?" Michael asked the dog.

"Woof!" said the dog as he and Josiah faded from his sight.

EPILOGUE

And so, the days of guests reporting odd sights and sounds at Southern Oak came to an end. Oh, every once in a while, someone passed along a report to Isabel, but those were just the suggestible types who knew the history of the manor. Isabel found that she missed the Estate as it once was. She would be happy never to repeat that harrowing drive with Mr. and Mrs. Daniels away from the shadows, but had enjoyed hearing the reports from guests over the years. For a time she threw herself into researching James Alden Ward and added to the record of the Estate. She also revised the script for the ghost tour and included his grave which now had a special marker added with his real name and a short explanation. John Fairchild had buried him in haste and left the grave unmarked, but Lydia's Aunt Cordelia suggested that there might be a need to locate it in the future. It was she who created the false name. This interesting bit of information came to light when Isabel located letters written to Cordelia Fairchild from the family attorney.

She remained in touch with the Daniels and updated them on her findings. The Daniels had taken Phoebe's advice and booked a long weekend in early October to see the fall colors. She was looking forward to seeing them again and planned to tell them about her decision to resign her position after the new year. She had accepted a position with an inn in the Shenandoah Valley area, an inn with a certain reputation.

She also kept in touch with Lynda Fuller whom she now really did consider to be a friend rather than a business acquaintance. She learned that Steve had been able to relocate and be nearer to Lynda. Jobs as an IT tech are apparently in high demand and he was able to latch on to the library system's IT department. They were seeing one another and taking it slowly.

From Lynda she learned that Keith was still recovering from his experiences. He had moved into his parents' home, just temporarily of course. Isabel couldn't find it in her heart to feel very sorry for him, but she wasn't surprised when Mr. Daniels indicated that he wished him well.

As for Michael Daniels, he might, once again, be guilty of keeping things from his wife. Sarah frequently mentioned how happy she was to have Michael back to his old self, so frequently in fact that he didn't see any need to correct her observations just yet.

Acknowledgements

WRITING A BOOK IS THE fun part. Proofreading and then proofreading again and again and still finding a need for corrections can become maddening. Fortunately, I had a flock of wonderful, patient readers who saw what my own eyes were unable to see.

Many thanks to Aleida Maron for her encouragement, feedback on content, and an eagle eye that spotted oh so many errors. Long-time friend, Tina Neville, was the first to suggest it as suitable to the cozy category of fiction and encouraged me to try the self-publishing route. My sister, Diane Snyder, provided yet another set of eyes and more of the encouragement she always provides in every situation. Childhood friend, Lynn Wilson, read with the eye of an editor and gave the spark of an idea that moved things in a slightly different direction. I also shared it with several others who provided enough "atta girls" to convince me, at last, to give it a go.

Without my husband this book would not exist. He provided the original spark, encouraged my writing, and helped me navigate the publishing platform. He carried out the final painstaking proofreading of the book to iron out those niggling formatting issues. His patience seemingly has no end. I am blessed to have him as a partner in life.

S. L. SUMNER

About the Author

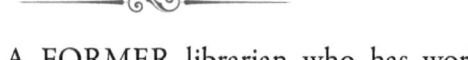

S.L. SUMNER IS A FORMER librarian who has worked in schools and libraries. When she isn't writing she likes to curl up with one or both of her delightful terriers and a good book.

In 8th grade her English teacher had the class keep a journal for a grading period. When it was returned the teacher wrote: "When you're a writer I'll collect your books." She never forgot those words and hopes that the reader will enjoy her efforts as much as Mrs. DePaula once did. *Dearly Beloved* is her first book.